BROKEN

BROKEN

THE GIRL IN THE BOX
BOOK SIX

Robert J. Crane

BROKEN

THE GIRL IN THE BOX, BOOK SIX

Robert J. Crane
Copyright © 2013 REIKONOS PRESS
All Rights Reserved.

Contact Robert J. Crane via email at
cyrusdavidon@gmail.com

Acknowledgments

Here's my grateful thanks to all those who helped me get this book out the door (it's a metaphorical door; I don't think there were any actual doors involved) and into your hands (and now I'm mixing metaphors. I'm a great writer!) In no particular order:

Carien Keevey - for pints of Guinness, great conversation, and an excellent read on this book.

Kea Grace - who persevered to finish her readthrough in record time, in spite of countless paws on the keyboard trying to keep her from it.

Paul Madsen - for finding about a billion and a half errors that I carefully inserted into my manuscript just to see if he'd notice. Hah! I'm kidding. They call them errors for a reason, after all.

Sarah Barbour - for making room in her schedule to get this done unannounced, and her always-careful attention to detail.

Karri Klawiter - for one hell of an awesome cover. Once again, she takes the vaguest of ideas from me and turns it into awesomesauce (which is like applesauce, but wholly better).

Finally to my parents, my wife and my kids. Who loves ya, baby? Not Telly Savalas, I can tell you that much. No, it's me.

One

When I awoke, it was sunny in the room, bright, blissfully so. There was a smell of pancakes wafting in the air, the sweet, lovely flavor of the griddle filling my nose and my taste buds, as though the syrup were already waiting for me out in the kitchen. I let out a sigh of contentment, and gave a slow stretch—from top to bottom, one of those stretches that starts in the shoulders and expands in both directions to the tips of my fingers and all the way down to every toe. I felt lazy, satisfied, and I couldn't quite place my finger on the reason why I felt so content until I heard him sigh next to me.

"Good morning," I said, giving him a kiss. Not even a taste of morning breath came from him, even when I parted his lips and went for some tongue. I felt adventurous and the sleepy drowse that still enveloped me couldn't hide the stir of other cravings besides the ones in my stomach. His hair felt luxurious as I ran my fingers through it.

"Morning," he replied, his voice reassuring for reasons that escaped my immediate grasp. Zack. My rock. My first love. His dirty-blond hair wasn't mussed by the bed at all; at least no more than it was on a daily basis. "Sleep well?" His coffee-brown eyes stared back into mine and there was just a moment's hint of something disturbing, but it passed, something between a memory and a nightmare.

"Yes," I somehow found the answer, even though I wasn't sure. The smell of pancakes was still heavy in the air, and my eyes adjusted as I took in the room around me. It was my room, in the house where I'd grown up. There was a memory of something else, but I couldn't quite land on it. I shuffled my gaze from the old, worn, almost orange-stained dresser covering one wall to the little stand that sat next to the door. My bed was in the corner, pushed up against the wall. "I don't even remember dreaming."

"That's good, right?" He rolled to get out of bed, naked, and I watched. He shot a backward look. "It's impolite to stare."

"Though fairly common nowadays," I teased as he knelt to fish through a pile of clothes. I rolled over and grasped at the curtains, pulling them back to take a look. There was a flash of snow before I blinked the brightness out of my eyes, and saw the green grass outside through the clear window. I thought I remembered there being an armoire in front of this window, not a bed. It was almost a memory I could grasp, but after a moment it seemed far away and insignificant, totally unimportant now. I turned to look back at the naked man who had been rooting around for clothes on my floor to find him fully dressed now, staring back at me with empty eyes. "Hey," I said. He did not respond. "Hello?" I waved a hand in front of him. "Hey."

"'Hey' yourself," came a voice from the door, and I looked around Zack to see my mother standing in the doorframe. "Your breakfast is getting cold."

"Breakfast?" I frowned. "You cook?"

"Smartass," she said with a roll of the eyes. "I made pancakes and ramen noodles."

"Oh, good, I'm hungry," I said, and meant it. I glanced to Zack as I walked toward the door. "Follow me, dear."

As I passed through the door, the world opened up around me, and I was in a bright place, with glass all around, stretching up two-story walls to a higher level above us. I looked at the table. It was the only thing in focus; everything else was hazy, but familiar. "Come on," Mom said, gesturing to a plate at the table. "Meatloaf and coffee."

"But I don't like …" The smell of pancakes was gone, but my

stomach still rumbled at the new aroma, though there was something vaguely abhorrent about it.

"Come on," Mother said again, "your friends are all waiting." She motioned at my chair, and for the first time I realized that there were others around the table with her. I took a tentative step forward and found myself in the seat, my meal staring up at me, all brown and somehow both appealing and unappealing at the same time.

"You don't like what I've made for you," Mother's voice rang out, and I looked up to see her face twist with scorn. "You really are an ungrateful child, you know. Eat what you're given, then ask for more. That's what you do when you're being polite."

"Yes, Mother," I said, and there was a fork in my hand. I looked to my left and saw Reed, my brother—half-brother, anyway—his dark hair around his shoulders, his suit an odd, glowing white. "Aren't you going to eat anything?" I asked him.

"Nothing for me, thanks," Reed said, and I saw a glass of water appear in his hand as he sipped it coolly. "I only eat Italian food lately."

"I'll eat whatever I can get," came a voice from next to him. I leaned forward and saw a shock of blond hair as Kat Forrest leaned forward so I could see her. Her green eyes glistened with an almost malicious light. "Older is better, though."

"That's … awkward," I replied. "Did I just say that out loud? I meant it, I think."

"Yeah, I end up saying stuff out loud that I shouldn't, too," came the voice from next to her. My eyes followed along the edge of the table, and another face came into focus, darker complexioned, with curly, dirty-blond locks. "Gets me into trouble sometimes."

"I can't imagine how that could possibly happen," Reed chimed in, sipping his water.

"Me either," Scott replied from his place next to Kat. His

complexion looked washed out and he was perspiring so heavily I could see the water drip down his face. "I keep on doing it, though."

"Freud would say you're simply manifesting thoughts of the sort you would like to see spoken aloud," came the voice of the man seated between Scott and my mother. His dark skin was strangely muted in the bright light of the glass room around us, the painful sunlight blotting out much of the detail. "In doing so, you're giving your subconscious a chance to express its desires."

"Huh," Scott said, at rapt attention. "What do you think my subconscious is saying?"

"That is an excellent question," Dr. Zollers said, with a coffee mug in his hand, his eyes on mine as he answered. "If I were Freud, I'd tell you that it probably means that you want to kill your father and take your mother as your wife."

There was the screech of chair legs skidding against the floor as Scott stood up. "I don't have to take this from you," he said, his face twisted in outrage. A moment later his face went slack, any sign that he was upset disappearing as though it had never been there. "I guess I better get to work on that if I want to be married by fall, huh?"

"Attaboy," Reed said, taking another slow sip of water. "Keep living up to everyone's expectations of you. That's the way to do it."

"He never lived up to mine," Kat said with a dismissing wave. "In any area." She eyed Dr. Zollers. "But you ... you look old ... er."

Zollers hid his expression behind his coffee cup, but I caught the hint of an eyeroll.

"Your friends are lovely, dear," my mother said, focusing on the plate in front of her. She took a bite of pancakes heavy with maple syrup, and I could almost taste it over the chorus of meatloaf clashing with bitter, strong coffee that had no sweetness whatsoever. "I wish I'd had a chance to meet them all."

"You didn't?" I mumbled, looking around. "Who's missing?"

"The big one," she replied, the pancakes gone from in front of her. She had a sword laying before her now. "You know, Erich. Winter." She paused. "The one who … well, you know. Him."

I frowned, and something prickled at the back of my mind. The bright light around us dimmed, then disappeared. I looked around the table in a rush; to my left, Reed had vanished and so had Kat and Scott. I blinked at mom, who still sat there. "Where did everybody go?"

"On," she said, fingering the grip of the katana that lay on the table between us. "They left without you."

"Oh," I said. "Well, I don't want to be alone—"

"You always have been," my mother's voice came in a chilling reply as the room darkened further.

"What do you think?" I cocked my head and looked to Dr. Zollers, who remained across from me, his coffee in his hand, coolly watching me.

"I think it's a dream, Sienna," he said, and his features were not nearly as blurry as the others.

"Other than that."

He pursed his lips and looked to the side, and there was a metric ton of regret waiting when he looked back at me. "I think you're going to be awake very, very soon, and that when you do, you'll find more than your share of troubles waiting for you, as usual. I think that you've passed the point of retreat, and that you're going to have to deal with all of it now, every single thing you've been putting off. For that I'm sorry." His mouth became a thin line, a grimace, and he looked down. "And even sorrier that you have to do it alone—but unfortunately, I can't stay any longer—"

I blinked and he was gone, and it was just my mother and I, with the sword between us. "I told you that you weren't ready," she said with a shrug. "I told you he was using you like a puppet."

"Who?" I asked.

The light came back, outside the glass, faint, and I could see snow on the ground, as far as the horizon. It was a painfully gray day from the sky above to the horizon line, clouds covering every inch of sky. "You know." My mother gestured to the world outside the glass walls. Flurries came down from above and the glass turned white with a sudden, icy accumulation. I heard the windows freeze and crack, straining like the time last year I had walked on the frozen surface of a pond after it had started to melt—

"Winter." She brought her gaze back to me. "I'm sorry I couldn't meet all your friends." She looked to my right, stared with a finger in her mouth for a moment, then leaned in closer to me. "That one doesn't seem quite right, daughter of mine. Are you sure he's ... well?"

I turned, slowly, to Zack, who was still sitting next to me. He was staring blankly ahead, his tanned face white, white as though the snows had covered him. His pupils were unmoving, and the light was out of the coffee-brown eyes. I looked down into the mug in my hand and it was in there, the same color his eyes had once been, but when I looked back his were shut, and the table was gone, and I was sitting, my knees around my chin. It was a field, and snow was coming down around me, and Zack lay, eyes open, stretched out over the cold ground—

Two

I didn't scream, but only because I was still in the grip of the paralysis of sleep. I came to in the box, the smell of it heavy in the air, hard metal against my back and pinching at my toes in front of me. I jerked my head up from where it had been slumped forward, my neck lolling as I came back to wakefulness. The smell was foul; I didn't know how long I had been in the box, but it had been days, days in which I'd only left occasionally, when needed, to drink, to eat, but not to shower. My body smelled foul, every inch of it, and I didn't care. I took a breath, and the air within hit my tongue, stagnant, almost stained with the stench. I braced myself against the wall and let the back of my head hit metal, a quiet thunk that I repeated twice more, trying to trade pain for clarity.

When my head cleared, everything—my memory of all that had happened that had brought me here—rushed back and I wished I my brain was still shrouded in fog. My dream had seemed so much better than the reality. My mouth was dry, and I smacked it open and shut twice.

Need to drink soon, came the quiet, rasping voice in my head. *Little doll is slowly wasting away.*

"Your concern is touching," I rasped myself, more from a scratchy throat than anything. "In fact, why don't you take your touching concern and go touch yourself with it? Over and over, preferably."

No need to get so nasty with Wolfe.

"I thought nasty was how you liked it." I could feel him, the first to stir, but the others were coming to life now, too. I didn't care. They were bastards, all of them. Well, all but one of them.

Bastards who talked and talked and talked at me all day long, from when I woke up to when I fell asleep, all but the one I wanted to talk to me. He had been nothing but silent.

Wolfe thinks you should—

"Don't care."

The darkness is insufferable, came the thick, Norwegian accent of Bjorn.

"You're from Norway, aren't you? Isn't it dark like twenty hours a day there in the winter? Deal with it." How did he speak in an accent in my head? Dipshit.

We should leave this place, Bjorn said, *leave it behind, go find Janus—*

"No."

There came a third voice, more reasonable, if slightly pleading. My sister, Klementina. *She lives—*

"Not if I get hold of her, that traitorous bitch."

—she still breathes—

"I could fix that."

—and now she remembers—

"She is not your sister." I let the rage fuel me, thinking of the blond-haired demon who had sold the Directorate out to Omega, thought of how she hid behind Janus until he told her to come out, like a good little— "You said yourself there's nothing of Klementina left in Kat." I exhaled hard, forceful, angry. "Nothing left but an Omega shell now. A puppet."

But we could—

"No." I ran a hand down my cheek, felt the stiffness in the skin, as though it had salted over. "I don't wanna leave."

Wolfe warned you—

"So helpful. Seriously. Go touch yourself."

—warned you that Janus was different than the others that had come before.

"Yet not a word about Erich Winter. Go figure."

There are things in motion, Bjorn spoke inside me, *things happening the whole world over for our people, things that will redefine our race—*

I waved a hand at him as though he were a fly I could shoo away, and I tucked my head down and ran a finger through my frizzed, tangled hair. "And I told you I don't care." I paused. "Or at least I told one of you I don't care. Just assume I'm speaking to all of you when I say something, because I want nothing to do with any of you friggin' convicts that are imprisoned in my brain." I took a breath through my nose and nearly gagged. When I got control of my breathing again, I took shallow breaths through my mouth. "If I had it my way, I'd empty you all out, and my own brain, too." In a flash, I thought of a gun, of what it could do for me—

There was only a second's silence before Wolfe spoke into the void. I could sense the terror of all three of them, scared shitless at the prospect of me killing myself—and them by default, for a second time. *Little doll, so natural to have these feelings after what you've been through—*

"And you'd know how? Other than because you caused them in others over and over throughout your sick, pathetic life?" I looked up, as though I could see him standing over me while I spoke. "Watching other people have emotions, feelings, loving and caring doesn't make you an expert by some sort of study or proxy, you psychopath."

Not helpful, though, Little Doll, Wolfe went on. *Wolfe watched, Wolfe saw, Little Doll is right—*

"I have a name, you ass."

—Wolfe inflicted more pain and death than Wolfe can speak of, he said, and his voice was smooth and plying. *But Wolfe saw pain, and Wolfe knows pain, has lived in pain like the Little Doll is feeling.*

"Bull," I laughed. "Bullllllllshiiiiiiiiiit."

There was a flash in my head, of something that happened long ago, far away, on another continent, and it was followed by a seering sense of loss, of agony. I felt bile well up in the back of my mouth and I wanted to heave—again. *Wolfe is not a liar.*

"Just a murderer, rapist and torturer," I said, leaning my head back against the inside of the box. There were eyes in the darkness, their eyes, peering at me. "Forgive me for failing to make *that* subtle distinction."

Wolfe has been through what the doll is going through, and the pleading was gone, I could feel the heat of his emotions now, he was feeding me the vision—of a house, with a family, screaming in pain, the air thick with the smell of a stew, and then blood everywhere, and the agonizing pain of loss, of heartbreak. I nearly vomited as a flash gave me a vision of a snowfield outside, a lone figure lying in the middle of it with flakes coming down around him. I felt a burning in my chest at the memory. *Wolfe knows how to make it better.*

"*I* know how to make it better," I said, resting my head on my palm. The weight of my skull was intense, and I wondered if my wrist could hold it up, it was so heavy. "I told you, I just take a pistol and—"

No no no no no—A chorus of the voices lifted up, and I heard just a hint of one far away, the one I wanted to hear, as though he were on the distant edge of a crowd, shouting to me across it. I tried to look for him, but it was as though I levered myself up, and by the time I did so, he was gone, slipped out of sight.

Zack.

Wolfe knows how to ease the loss, to ... salve the pain.

"Please, tell me this is a solution that involves cannibalism," I said with a disgruntled laugh. "Because I could use some humor in my day." I looked around soberly. "Actually, I am hungry. If you ruin that with a tale of human flesh being eaten, I will never forgive you."

No no no, Little Doll, nothing so dirty, I caught the hesitation in the way he said it and I knew he was putting on the show for me. Still, I listened because although I kind of didn't want to, I kind of did. *Age-old remedies for these sorts of wrongs, you know, older than anything, the idea of what to do when someone makes you hurt, makes you suffer. Little Doll, you are stronger than you know—*

"And yet you keep calling me a little doll," I said with a sigh.

—stronger than anyone knows. And the Little Doll knows what she could do, but maybe ... is afraid to do it. I could almost sense him looking around in my head, as though drawing on the support of those around him, his fellow prisoners. *But we ... we three ... we have all done it. Have all done things to those who wronged us, can be ... guides for the Little Doll who isn't a murderer ... who doesn't want to hurt anyone—*

"Oh, I want to hurt someone."

That's good.

"It's really not," I said, almost choking on the words.

They hurt you. Hurt you worse than anything. Only one way to make that better, to cure yourself of the pain, Little Doll. And Wolfe can show you, oh yes, he can—

"Ugh."

He is not wrong, Gavrikov said.

"Listen to the voice of reason. The guy who wanted to blow up the entire city of Minneapolis to spare everyone the pain of living."

It is natural to want to hurt someone back, when you've been hurt. When my father turned on me and my sister, I—

"Thanks for the input."

Blood answers blood, Bjorn said within me. *There is only one response to what they have done to you.*

"Says you."

Little Doll, the voice came again, cloying, preying. *Wouldn't it feel good? They hurt you so ... wouldn't it just be right to make them pay, just a little?* I felt something within me stir. *Why wouldn't that make sense? Wouldn't it just be ... fair? To make them pay for leaving him like ... that.* I gasped and a vision of Zack, dead, staring up at me, flashed in front of my eyes, and my breathing picked up, quick breaths in and out, almost hyperventilating.

Soothing, Little Doll, long breaths, slow, in and out. I took the advice of the words in my ear, and my breathing began to slow as I calmed. *Yes, that's it. Like that. Think of them, and you get ... riled. But think of what you could do to them to repay them, and slow down, savor it, breathe it in slowly ...*

I didn't want to listen, but I did. There was an agony inside, a clashing cymbal and drums playing in my ears, and I kept seeing that moment, their faces, the ones who had done this.

His face, weathered and old. I had trusted him.

"I'm not a murderer."

They are, came Gavrikov's voice again. *They did this to you. Against your will. Forced you to ... the cruelest thing anyone could ever—*

They deserve it, Bjorn said. *He pretended to be your friend, they all did, and then, in a moment, they turned on you, took advantage of you, used your own body to perpetrate a horror upon him and yourself—*

He will never be able to leave you now, Wolfe said, and I felt a stir in the back of my head from Zack at that—a stir, and nothing more. *They've saddled you with the proof of their horrific betrayal for now and all time, so cruel a thing to do to such an innocent sweetness like the Little Doll ... made her trust them, fed her and pretended to love her, and then—*

It was as though I could hear a snap in my head, of fingers or something else, and then the darkness around me turned red, tinged with crimson. I took long, slow breaths, but they weren't relaxing, they were seething. I saw them all, one by one—

Parks. His long, gray hair and beard, my woolly mentor.

Clary. Stupid idiot. Rocks for brains and skin.

Eve. Colder than even Winter. Hated me. Always had, I think.

Bastian. Led them all. Let it happen. Talked Parks into doing it.

And Winter. I felt a flare of heat at the thought of him. He was ice and had been for as long as I had known him. I wanted to melt him, to draw some emotion out of him, to make him cast aside that glacial exterior, hear the flames lick at him, hear him scream the way Zack had—

There was a silence in my head. I knew they were there, still, in the back, waiting. "All right," I said, breathing, seething. "All right, yes. I want them to hurt. I want them to suffer like I suffered." I felt my teeth grind together. "But I can't do this by myself. I can't—" I flinched, in the darkness, in the box. "I don't know how to—"

So easy, came the rasp of Wolfe again. *So simple. The Wolfe can help, oh yes, he can. And the others, too, he added hastily, can help the Little Doll take her first steps into this new, brave, bad world, her first steps into the one that we have walked in since long before the Little Doll was even born ... experienced guides, oh yes.* I could almost feel Bjorn and Gavrikov nodding with him, and as much as that should have chilled me, it didn't. I felt a vague sense of relief, as though I were finally doing ... something. Anything. Other than sitting here, wallowing in misery.

But the Little Doll will have to find them first, Wolfe said, and I heard the eagerness. *Can the Little Doll do this?*

"Yes," I said after a long pause, and my voice almost cracked. "Yes. But I'm going to need ... a little more help."

Three

The bar was dark when I walked in, and a faint neon glow from a hundred different beer signs that hung on the walls painted the room. The bouncer inside the door looked me up and down with a wary eye and beckoned. I handed him my driver's license—or one with my picture on it, anyway, a spare I kept at my house along with an additional FBI I.D. and some other papers in case of an emergency. There was a scent of something being fried in the air, and the bouncer looked at me with smoky eyes, to my license, then back to me. He shrugged and handed it over. I walked on past him without even a breath of care. If he hadn't let me pass, it would have been his problem, not mine.

The room I walked into consisted of multiple levels divided into sections by rails and booths. I could see a dance floor somewhere in the distance, but there were enough mirrors on the walls that I wasn't entirely sure where in the building it was. I also did not care. The music blasting out of speakers overhead had way too much electronic noise in it for me to really consider it music, and the speaker system wasn't doing it any favors either, at least not to my metahuman ears. Besides, my eyes had settled on who I was looking for as soon as I walked in; everything else was ancillary noise at this point.

"Hey, pretty girl," a guy said, stepping into my path as I made my way toward the bar. The alcohol on his breath said he'd had at least twelve beers. "How about we—"

I let my left hand loose without really thinking about it, and it arced from my side in a quick motion and slapped him open-handed in the groin. All the air rushed out of him and he hit his knees. "How about we don't," I said as I walked past him and turned the corner to enter the section of the room that had the actual bar in it. I heard the murmured assent of voices around me, both in my head and out of it.

I took the last few steps up to the bar and didn't bother to take off my heavy wool coat, the one that was black and fell all the way to my knees. It was cold outside, now; the first breaths of winter infusing the air, and I didn't even feel any desire to remove it now that I was indoors. I went to the end of the bar, to the man who sat there, drinking a beer from a glass big enough to qualify as a bucket in most jurisdictions. He watched me the whole way over, trying not to act like he cared, but he stopped watching as I turned the last corner of the bar and came to the stool next to him. "Mind if I sit down?" I asked.

"If I say no, are you gonna do to me what you did to the last guy?" He was big, his face carried acne scars and a world of uncaring seeped out of his voice. He was chomping on a big cigar, unlit.

"Probably worse," I said, and took the seat next to him.

"Have a seat, then," he said, and pulled the cigar out of his mouth. "Welcome to my home away from home." Kurt Hannegan stared back at me from the next barstool, his massive frame dwarfing mine. "How'd you find me?"

I didn't answer for a minute. "He … told me you hang out here. That … he … had been here with you before."

There was a splash of uncertainty on his already surly face. "Yeah. Once or twice he was, I suppose. What are you doing here?"

I watched him as he took a long pull from his beer. "You heard?"

He finished the mug in one long drink and made a gesture to the bartender for another. "I heard."

"How?"

A new glass made its way to in front of him, and the barman asked politely if I wanted anything. I shook my head and he disappeared again. "Jackson told me," Hannegan said. "He and a couple other guys heard from Clary. Said the big man told the story loud and boisterous all the way up til the last part. Then he got quiet and needed booze and prompting to get to the finish." Kurt shot me a sidelong look. "So do you hear him now?" He pointed to his head. "Is he … with you … right now?

"Not so much, no," I said. "Kinda quiet for some reason."

There was the faintest look of amusement that vanished with his next gulp. "Yep," he put the glass down, "I'd be quiet, too, if I was stuck in my wife's head." His face froze in a look of horror or wistfulness; I didn't know which. As per usual lately, I didn't care, either.

"You haven't asked me why I'm here." I waited for him to turn and look at me but he stayed still on his stool. One hand stayed in front of him playing with a cardboard coaster that had been worn through with the perspiration from his beer. The other was anchored to his glass's handle and he fingered it, knuckles twitching as though he wanted to lift it one second, then didn't know what to do in the next. "Ask me, Kurt. Ask me why I'm here."

"Doesn't take a rocket scientist to know why you're here—"

"Which you aren't, anyway," I said.

"I'm not stupid—"

"That's open to some debate."

He didn't look at me. "You're mad. I would be, too—"

"I'm not mad," I said evenly. "I just want them dead."

He froze in place, his beer halfway to his mouth. "Yeah. That's kinda what I figured." He took a breath, holding the beer in place. "How do you figure to fit me into your plans?"

"You don't want them dead?" I asked him.

"I don't want to die," Hannegan answered, putting the beer

back down. "That's the only answer I care about, and me up against them is suicide, so I don't ask myself any of the other questions I might want to."

"I don't care if I die so long as they do, too," I said. There was not even a hint of reaction from him. "But I'm kinda in a rough spot here, because I'm out in the cold—"

"Everyone's in the cold with Winter."

"You know what I mean. I don't know his plans." My eyes narrowed at him. "Did you know?"

He looked at me sidelong for a second then went back to his beer, but I caught the hint of nerves. "What the hell kind of question is that? You think I'd be sitting in this bar from daybreak to closing every day if I knew this was coming—for you or ..." he looked around, as though someone were listening, "... him?"

"I dunno, Kurt," I said, and let the ice leak into my voice, "a week ago, a guy I would have said I trusted with my life ordered his flunkies to hold me down while they used my body to kill the only man I've ever loved. Not exactly feeling the trust flowing for anyone at the moment." I spun on the stool to face him. "Do you want Zack avenged or not?"

He took a long breath and pulled the cigar out of his mouth. "I got no loyalty to Winter." He gestured toward the door. "He offered me some work, to help guard him for a few weeks, and I told him to go f—" He let himself get carried away, but caught himself just in time. "Well, you know."

"Can you find out where he is?" I leaned in closer to him.

"Probably," Hannegan said, and looked me over. "But it's not gonna do you any good. M-Squad is still watching his back. They will pull you apart limb by limb before you get within a hundred feet of him. Which I don't think is gonna do Zack or you any damned good."

I reached into my coat pocket and pulled out a sheet of paper, a small one, and laid it on the bar. "Let me worry about that. I just need to know …" I let my finger trace along the paper, "… details. Everything you can get me. There's no way their security is flawless. All I need is some help finding the holes in it."

"It's not a piece of Swiss cheese." He glanced at the paper, then stared, almost slack-jawed, before slowly turning back to me with a faint nod of acknowledgment. "You're pulling out all the stops."

"I owe them," I said and stood up, slapping a roll of hundred dollar bills down on the bar—some of my savings from my year of working for Old Man Winter. Blood money, all of it. "I want to pay."

Kurt looked at me as he put the unlit cigar back in his mouth. "Don't you mean you want them to pay?"

"That's going to happen, too—I guarantee it." I stretched, my back still slightly stiff from the box I had left only an hour or so earlier. "And it'll be fun. And satisfying." I eyed him, the big man on the stool, and he suddenly seemed incredibly small. "But you don't get anything for free. No, I'll pay." I gave him a slight smile as I turned to walk away, one that I actually felt; cold, brutal, mean. "But every one of them is going to pay first."

Four

It was night, and my stomach growled at me as I crawled through a patch of wet dirt outside Hastings, Minnesota. The ground had thawed after a day of sun, a day in which I didn't know what to do with myself because it followed the night I had met Kurt in the bar. It was muddy now, as muddy as I'd ever seen it, and my elbows and hands were covered in it, thick mud that stank a little of sulfur. I kept myself low as I approached the farmhouse; I had belly-crawled through the grass all the way from the highway. I would have preferred to do what I was going to do from a distance, with a rifle, but I didn't have one of those. I felt the weight of my gun and holster pushing against my ribcage, angrily poking at me as it brushed the ground. Kurt had gotten it for me, and like so many things the big man had introduced into my life, it brought some pain with it.

I ignored it. Pain was good. Pain was my friend. The pain kept me crawling on as the night deepened. It was after midnight, now, and I was approaching the farmhouse after crawling for hours. I was going as slowly as I dared, my patience strained but not breaking because of what I had to do. There were about a million stars hanging over me, the only light save for a porch light that was about a hundred yards away from me and getting closer as I went. I was making as little noise as possible, almost none, and there was no noise of crickets to mask my approach. I hoped I was being quiet enough, because I didn't want this to get loud before I was ready. I wanted to get close-up. Personal.

I wanted it that way, but I didn't want it that way, either.

This is the way it should be, Little Doll.

"Thanks for giving your opinion," I whispered. "I shall cherish this advice always, and file it away with all the other fun memories you've given me, like that time you … oh, right. We've never had any good times together, only misery."

He mercifully shut up as I kept going. I knew before I'd started that I was in for a long night of this. I had started hours ago and miles away on a back road where I left my car (Zack's car) parked. From what Kurt had told me, I was guaranteed to find my target at home. Apparently he never left anymore, not for anything. The tire tracks in the muddy driveway told me others had been here recently. The single page Kurt had included in the package he left on my doorstep along with the gun said it was pizza deliveries, sandwiches, occasionally groceries, and booze. The booze truck came every other day, and the credit card receipts indicated some heavy drinking being done at the house I was looking at.

Good. I hoped it was still going on. Drunkards are easier to catch by surprise. It's hard to pay full attention to the world around you when you're busy getting hammered.

And in this case, I needed all the help I could get.

I reached the end of the tall grass that surrounded the farmhouse in all directions. If this had been a working farm at one point, it was in the distant past now. Now it was a near-abandoned house less than an hour south of Minneapolis and St. Paul, aged and damned near forgotten. That is, at least by everybody but me, the lone occupant of the place, some food delivery drivers and whoever dropped off five gallons of vodka every other day.

I peered out of the grass, trying to keep my face hidden as I looked at the windows, the lights shining brightly within. Every light in the place seemed to be on, and I wondered for a flash if that was due to drunken forgetfulness or as some sort of lure. I saw a shadow move in the window, a figure cross to the kitchen from the living room, and realized it wasn't much of a trap if so.

My target was in sight. I didn't even deign to think of him as a person anymore, just a target to be filled with bullets, as though I were at the range.

It was how he would have wanted me to see it. It was how he trained me.

I watched Glen Parks close his refrigerator door, his bushy gray beard hanging in front of him as he plodded back toward the living room. He disappeared out of sight with a bottle in his hand, the bright yellow label obvious against his weathered hand, and I breathed a sigh of relief. He did appear to be drinking. That was good news for me.

I ignored the smell of the mud as I got to my feet. I crept forward across the driveway, sticking to the shadows as I ducked behind the old, rust-covered pickup truck that was in the driveway, parked about ten feet from the back door. I pondered entry points the way he'd taught me. Somewhere about twenty feet away from me, there was a sound of a blaring TV, loud enough that I could hear it from where I was standing. I estimated he was somewhere close to it, probably no more than twenty-five feet from where I was crouched, just a wall or two and some windows separating us. The volume of the TV was a good sign for me, likely to drown out not only my approach but also at a high enough volume to mask the sound of my entry, if I did it right.

I took a breath, thankful that once again the idiots in my skull were being quiet. I knew how to force entry to a property, knew how to approach quietly, knew how to get myself within close range of him. My only challenge was going to be the moment of truth, the second where I had to pull the trigger. That was where I had always failed before. Not at the range, where it counted for nothing, but in the moment when I needed to take a life.

And for this one, I needed to cut that hesitation out, because there wasn't any time for it at all. Parks was a canny bastard, and even with the steps I'd taken to make this work, I wouldn't have much time to act before he did. His response was impossible to predict, which was why I needed to fill his skull with bullets before he got a chance to employ whatever contingency plan he might have.

I kept low as I made my way to the back door. I felt a flash of hesitation as I reached for the handle; if it was locked, I needed to break it down and breach in seconds. Based on where I'd seen him go after he grabbed the vodka, the moment I was through the door I would have a clear shot at him in the corner of the next room. All I had to do was crash through the door with my left shoulder, aim right, and start pulling the trigger. I didn't have any flashbangs, but I doubted they would have helped with Parks anyway; he'd been the one that taught me how to acclimate to them and he'd be ready and moving the minute he saw one come through the door.

No, my best bet was to come in firing, aim fast, shoot fast, and pump him so full of lead that he was unresponsive when I came to deliver the coup de grace. He had to be just sitting in an easy chair in the corner of the room; I could almost sense it based on where I'd seen him go. It's not like he knew I was coming, after all—this was coming as an absolute surprise. I reached for the door handle with my left hand and felt my palms sweat as I grabbed the Walther out of my coat with the right. I held it up, hefted it, the weight in my hand almost insignificant. I took a deep breath and inhaled the scent of the mud, the gun oil, my own sweat. I would have preferred something bigger, with more rounds in the magazine, but I had what Kurt gave me and that was it.

At least I had plenty of bullets. I would probably need them before this was all over.

I heard a slight squeak as I touched the handle. It was unlocked, I realized as I rolled it halfway down. It made an almost imperceptible noise, and I hoped that the TV was blocking it. I hit the door hard with my shoulder and it burst open as I threw myself in, my gun already aiming through the passage from the kitchen to the living room where I'd seen him last. Time seemed to slow down as I burst into the world of the farmhouse, with its old white plaster walls. Ahead of me, at the end of the house was an empty chair, and all around it were small monitors lit with white.

Security monitors covering every angle around the house and exterior, I realized in a breathtaking moment of kicking myself. The chair was empty, the old, ragged red thing abandoned, its master nowhere in sight.

I heard the subtle sound of a safety coming off a weapon just behind my left ear, and then a barrel prodded me in the back of the head—only once, and then he backed out of my reach. "Put it on the ground and slide it away, slow. Just like I taught you— consider it a test." His voice dragged, only slurring a little—not nearly drunk enough for me to beat him on the draw. "You've got til the count of three, and then I'm gonna pepper my wall with your brains. And you know—*you know*—unlike you, I'll actually do it."

Five

I ground my teeth as I lay my pistol down exactly as he had said and slid it across the room.

"Got a backup?" he asked, leaning against the kitchen wall a good ten feet from me. Not close enough for me to get to him before he cut me in half with a shotgun blast. I kept my head turned away from him, still looking at the red easy chair I had sworn he would be in. I should have known better. Should have suspected something. Parks was paranoid. I should have assumed he'd have claymore mines wired on every door and window, video security hidden all around the perimeter, motion sensors and every trick I could imagine (and a few I couldn't) to keep his personal security inviolate.

I cursed myself; I had let the ragged farmhouse and my desire to get this over with sway some of the operational instincts he had burned into me like a brand on my skin. "No backup," I said. "I wouldn't be carrying a Walther as my primary if I'd had something higher caliber."

"This is what happens when you lay an operation on too quick and you've got too much personal stake in the outcome," he said, lecturing me, still slurring only a little. "You got hasty, impatient. Should have done more scouting. If you'd been on your game and cased the place in the daylight, you would have seen the places where I hid the video surveillance and the motion sensors." He sniffed. "I saw you before you even got out of your car, before you started crawling across the muddy ground. I thought I'd given you situational awareness that could beat what you'd find in professional soldiers." His face fell only a little. "I thought I taught you better than that."

"Did you?" I asked, keeping my hands up in the air, not looking at him. "I don't remember."

"Don't give me that," he snarled, sounding much like the animal I knew he was. "You know better than to do it like this. You tried to breach my back door. *Mine*. If I hadn't unhooked the claymore before you got in here, it woulda turned you into stew meat!" I turned my head slightly right to look; sure enough, just above the frame rested a claymore mine, the small straps unplugged from ties where they attached to the door, the ultimate in home security. Anyone coming in through that door would die horribly, a spray of pellets propelled by an explosive charge turning their body to a mush like the ultimate shotgun blast.

"And I care why exactly?" I turned, slow, rising from my knees to face him.

He couldn't take a step back as he was already against the wall, but I saw a subtle change in his posture, as though he wanted to recoil but was hiding it. "Because you don't want to get killed."

"I don't care if I die," I said, staring him down. His eyes had always been somewhat warm before, at least to me; now they barely met mine and were coldly assessing. His pupils were beginning to dilate; I could see them even at this distance. "All I care about is making sure I settle accounts before I go."

I saw him start to reply to that, then stop. He kept the shotgun aimed at me, level with my head. A simple pull of the trigger would end it, I knew. The chorus in my head was silent, though I could feel their nervous emotion within. Strangely, I felt none of my own.

"Go on," I said. "You've got the gun, you've got me dead to rights. I'm in your house, I came to kill you—"

"You can't kill me—" He shook his head.

"You don't think so?" I asked, staring him down. I could feel it: he wanted to turn his gaze sideways, look away from me, but he couldn't. He wanted to avert his eyes, as though to give the little broken girl in front of him some privacy from the weight of the emotions I knew were oozing off me, but his training wouldn't let him look away from a potential threat. So he kept staring at me and I kept staring right back at him. I had nothing but accusation in my glare; his, in return, was fading.

"You shoulda approached faster," he said, and the slurring was getting worse. "Shoulda burst through the front of the house with a truck—"

"I didn't have a truck."

"Shoulda stolen one," he went on, swallowing heavily. "Break through the front of the house, odds are good you'd have taken me out before I could get clear. If not, the element of surprise would have been worth it. Or a sniper rifle from a distance—you always were a hell of a marksman—"

"I didn't want to do it like that," I said.

"Because you couldn't be bothered to plan it out like you should," he said, and I could see him starting to sweat, "you're sitting here staring down the barrel of a shotgun when you oughta be looking at my corpse from a half-mile away."

"It was never gonna be like that," I said calmly and took a step to my right, leaning against the kitchen counter. He swept the shotgun barrel to keep me covered. I had taken a step in the direction of my gun, and with the waggle of the barrel, I knew if I took another he was going to pull the trigger. I watched his eyes, and it was hard to know if that was an empty threat or if he was serious. I wasn't going to test it. "You know I have trouble killing people. Always have, ever since Gavrikov—"

"It's a weakness I would have trained out of you, sooner or later," he said, taking a hand off the barrel to wipe the perspiration off his forehead.

"It's funny," I said. "Because I killed Wolfe to save my own life, and I killed Gavrikov to save the city because I owed them for what Wolfe did. Do you know how many people he killed to get to me?" I watched as Parks shook his head, slowly. "Two hundred and fifty-four. Men, women, children. From those first two guys outside the supermarket to the last family he slaughtered before he came to get me in my own basement, he killed two hundred and fifty-four people. I remember the number. It echoes in my head." I felt something in my mind from Wolfe, a vague sense of glee, and ignored it.

"You didn't cause that," Parks said, and brushed the gray hair out of his eyes where it was starting to mat on his forehead. He blinked his eyes, twice, but the shotgun stayed level.

"I did, actually." I put my palms flat on the counter behind me, resting them in plain sight, where he could see them. "By my inaction, I caused those people to die. If I had stepped up sooner, some of them would still be alive. So I'm responsible." I turned my voice more chipper. "Like you, with Zack's death. You're responsible. You, Clary, Eve—I know she wasn't there, but let's be honest, she would have been involved in a heartbeat if she had been—Bastian, Winter … and me. You all took Winter's orders, and you carried them out, and let my power do its work. Zack's dead, the rest of us are all alive." My eyes narrowed. "I intend to correct that imbalance."

He let out a ragged breath. "You've already failed. Maybe if you'd planned better—"

"My plan's going just fine," I said coolly and looked to my right. The gun was still there. Out of reach.

He watched me eye the Walther and pulled up his grip on the shotgun, tightening the butt of it against his shoulder. "You've got a gun pointed at you after you failed to breach properly. If that was part of your plan, then I'm afraid I've misjudged you." He let out a long breath, and the gun swayed by millimeters as he did so. "You were my favorite student, the best pupil I ever—"

"Do you kill the lovers of all your best students?" I saw him blanch. "Or am I special?"

He let hang a moment of silence between us. "You're special all right. Or you were. Now you're so blinded with rage you can't even think straight enough to come up with an operational concept and carry it out with a clear head." He waved his hand at my pistol on the floor and then let it come back to mop the sweat pouring down his brow. "Whoever got that gun for you oughta get their ass kicked; all they did was set you up to commit suicide." He smacked his dry lips together again; they were dark in the low light of the kitchen, almost blue.

"I'll make sure to let Kurt know what you think of his efforts," I said.

"You have to analyze your target's weaknesses—"

"I know that," I snapped.

"Well, you didn't do it!" He looked like he was ready to yell again, but then a calm settled over him. Beads of sweat hung heavy on his forehead and I saw him open his mouth slightly, move his tongue around inside, then he blinked three times in rapid succession. "Oh. You did."

I watched him without flinching. "I did."

The shotgun lowered and he started to slump, falling down the counter until he rested on the floor, his back against the wall. "How?" His eyes were clouded, and then he nodded once in understanding. "The vodka."

"The vodka." I took slow, easy steps over to my pistol, where I stooped to pick it up. "You've been going through so much of it, once I sapped the delivery guy's memory it wasn't very hard to figure out which box was going to you. I saw you get one of the marked bottles from outside the window. The ones with the yellow label."

He gasped a little, his breathing unsteady, and he looked up at me. "How did you know I wouldn't kill you outright?"

I nodded. "It was a little bit of a risk, but this was the first test." I walked back over to him and put my foot on the barrel of his shotgun, pinning it to the floor, before I slid it out of his unresisting grasp. "The poison wasn't enough to kill you, by the way, even if you drank the whole bottle. You'd be fine in an hour or so, I'd guess. Metahuman metabolism works fast, you know."

He looked at me, his eyes half-lidded. "You picked me first?"

"I picked you first," I said quietly. "It had to be you first."

"Why?" It came out as little more than a gasp, his lips blue from the cyanosis that he was fighting against, the lack of oxygen getting to his brain from the poison I'd laced his vodka with.

"Because you were going to be the hardest." I watched his eyes, and they were warm again, even as I watched him struggle to stay conscious. The sweat was rolling off him now, dripping off his forehead and soaking his white t-shirt.

He smiled. "I'm a tough target. Taught you everything I know. Everything." His smile evaporated. "You really were my best student."

"I know," I said. "Which is why you had to be first."

"No," he said with a shake of his head. "I'm not helping Winter anymore. I told him to shove it, after …" he swallowed, "what happened. I told him he was on his own."

"I know," I said, squatting down across from him as I picked up the shotgun. "I heard about that."

"I never wanted to—" His whole face sagged, and I watched his tough facade deteriorate. "I never wanted to do what we did that night. But you …" He gasped, holding his chest, and I knew it must be agonizing. "You don't know how bad it's gonna be, what's coming. I wish … I wish I'd seen a better way, but I didn't." He blinked, and then his next words came out choked. "I wish I could make it right."

"You can't." I felt the bite when I said it. "Are there more guns in the basement?"

"Whole damned arsenal," he said with a faint smile,

struggling to get each word out.

"Any traps?"

"All the standard ones," he said, leaning his head against the cabinets. "You know how to get through 'em."

"I do," I said, "because I was your best student." I stood. "And that's why you had to be first."

He blinked, drowsy, and looked up at me. "I don't understand."

"You always taught me to take out the hardest target first." I stared down at him, knowing I couldn't allow myself to feel anything. I forced it all back, every feeling, every emotion, behind a wall.

He shook his head. "I'm not gonna be the hardest target. Not by a long shot. Old Man Winter ... he's got the others still looking out for him, at least one of them at all times, plus some of the agents that are left over—"

"I know," I said. "He's still not the hardest target." I pulled the pistol up from where it hung at my side and aimed it at him, staring at his face over the sights, the red dots lining up just below the spot between his eyes—exactly as he'd taught me to do it. It wavered a little in my hand as I did it. "This was always going to be the hardest thing I had to do."

There was a slow nod of realization from him as he stared back at me, not at the gun in my hand. "I'm glad it's you," he said, his voice cracking. "I'm glad it's going to be you, because another week of this and I would have done it myself."

I felt the tug of emotion on my face as I held the pistol level with his eyes, but I held it back. I felt my hand quiver, and the pistol shook. I looked down the sights at him, when I knew he had trained me to look at the front sight, to keep it in focus. At this range it didn't matter, but it was what I had been trained to do. "Is it supposed to be ..." I heard my voice crack. "Is it supposed to be this hard?"

I saw his face straighten, and his eyes were warm as he looked back at me, the instructor one last time. "It gets easier. Just—"

I focused on the front sight and his face blurred. My finger stroked the trigger once, then again in a double tap automatically, just like he'd taught me. Blood spattered my clothes, blending with the mud already caked on me, and I thought idly about how I'd never get either cleaned off, maybe ever again. I fired twice more to be sure he was dead, then felt my hand fall to my side after I re-safetied my pistol and then it automatically went back to the holster before I even realized it. That was a product of all his training, perfectly executed. I left the shotgun by the door as I walked out, each foot carrying me back toward the car; I'd need it to retrieve the weapons in the basement. I had no idea what I'd be heading into next and it always paid to be prepared for any situation. Someone had taught me that, once, a long time ago.

As I stepped out into the freezing air, I felt the tears I didn't even know I had shed turn cold on my cheeks.

Six

The light was bright around me, glaring through windows in spite of a gray sky, and I wondered if I was dreaming again. The world came slowly into focus, details emerging. There was a stone desk that looked like a rock mounted on wooden legs. Behind it sat a massive man who was nearing seven feet tall, his hair grayer than the sky behind him. The smell of leather from the chair I was seated in hung in the air. It felt new where my hands gripped the armrests. I looked around quietly, and saw Zack sitting to my side, his blond hair looking more mussed than ever. Old Man Winter sat across the desk from him.

"Ariadne told me you had some difficulty in apprehending the subject," Old Man Winter said, his voice a low rumble. I looked down and realized that it was as though I wasn't there, disembodied, a fly on the wall for a conversation between these two men. Winter's low timbre set my non-existent teeth to grinding, slow emotion rising as I tried to blink eyelids that weren't there and I tried to reconcile this memory of something I couldn't recall ever happening.

"Yeah," Zack said, and his whole body was uneasy, his posture tense. "Shouldn't Kurt be here for this? We went to her house to retrieve her together—"

"There is no need for me to speak to Kurt about this," Old Man Winter said with a simple wave of his hand. "His report and yours were exceptionally clear in the timing and execution of your entry into the house and subsequent pursuit to the grocery store."

"That was all Kurt," Zack said uneasily. "He managed to affix one of our pen trackers to the bumper of the car the girl—uh ...

Sienna, I think her name was—made her escape in."

"Her name is indeed Sienna," Old Man Winter said and, ponderously slow, he stood up then made his way to the window. There was snow on the ground beyond, covering the Directorate campus as I tried to fit this memory into my own. A slow realization had crept over me during the conversation; it had to have taken place right after Kurt and Zack had come to my house, after they had saved me from Wolfe the first time.

"We still have no idea who she was with when she was attacked or what the ..." his distaste was evident, "... thing that attacked her was—"

"His name is Wolfe," Old Man Winter said, "and he is very dangerous; Ariadne will ensure you see his file. I know you have not been working here long enough to have encountered someone with his scope of power."

"I've seen some pretty crazy things since I started working here," Zack said, filling the pause in the conversation.

"I have read your reports, reviewed your assignments," Old Man Winter said, looking back over his shoulder at Zack. "You have never seen anything like him."

"He ran," Zack said, with a shrug. "Ran from us, a couple humans armed with nothing more than tranquilizer guns, per your mission orders."

"There was surely more to it than that," Old Man Winter said. "Something you have not seen. Wolfe ... would not surrender something he was after so easily, and I very much doubt that a simple tranquilizer would give him any pause."

Zack shrugged again. "If you say so." He sat in quiet for a moment, his discomfort evident. "Is there ... anything else?"

"Yes," Old Man Winter said, turning back and returning to his seat, easing himself into the heavy chair as it squeaked at his weight. "The girl."

"The girl?" Zack frowned. "What about her?"

"She has been isolated for years," Old Man Winter said, "held captive by her mother. She will know little of the world, and now Wolfe—a meta of considerable power, a remnant of the old days of metahuman involvement in human affairs—has attempted to capture her. Another player of unknown origin has helped her to escape us. We know nothing of what she is standing in the middle of, but I know Wolfe, and if he is involved then she is important in some way."

Zack looked carefully at Old Man Winter. "Um, okay. I mean, she's here now, so we can protect her—"

"Protection is not all she will require," Old Man Winter said coldly, "assuming she accepts it. Her mother was strong-willed, difficult. I would expect the same from her and be pleasantly surprised if she was more … malleable. She will try to escape and eventually succeed, provided she is half as strong as Sierra. We must give her reasons to stay. Persuade her to cooperate until we can determine her purpose and powers."

The uneasiness that hung over Zack like a pall grew deeper. "I guess I can understand wanting to protect her until we can find out a little more of the mystery around her, but maybe if we were honest—"

"Honesty is not the best policy in a case such as this," Old Man Winter said, icy eyes staring at Zack. "Would you care to explain to a seventeen-year-old that she has unknown powers and is pursued by a man who is not a man at all but a mythical being who was once known as one-third of Cerberus, the hellhound? Some of this she will accept, but we have not enough answers to give. Honesty will not convince her to remain here, protected. We will need to give her … other reasons." There was never much emotion in anything Winter said, but there was something approaching wry amusement in the way he said it.

Zack stared at him blankly. "What … did you have in mind? I mean, there are other kids her age—"

"No," Winter said with a firm shake of the head. "None of them work for us; they are ... unreliable in this." Somehow he made the word *unreliable* sound like it was the worst thing that anyone could ever be.

"Unreliable for what?" Zack's face was slack yet expectant. He had no idea.

"From the housing record," Winter said, watching Zack carefully, "we can assume she has lived in the same home for something on the order of twelve years. From your report, it would appear that the girl has been isolated from the outside world, from exposure to others." He didn't blink, his cold blue eyes shining with a glow that was otherworldly. "She has had no friends, no family but her mother, who is best described as cold," Winter appeared to savor the hint of irony present in him calling someone else cold, "and has no romantic attachments."

Zack's mouth was slightly open, just short of agape. "That's tragic. But what do you want me to do about it?"

"I want you to give her a romantic attachment," Winter said bluntly.

"I'm sorry, what?" Zack blinked, and his head cocked slightly to the side.

"She will not know people," Winter said, "not truly. She has no connection with anyone. I want you to form a connection with her. Be friendly. Be more. Give her a reason to want to stay."

The gears were ratcheting in Zack's mind, it was obvious from the barely concealed disbelief written on his face. "You want me to ... pretend to be her friend?"

"No," Winter said, "I want you to genuinely be her friend. And if the opportunity arises, I want you try for more—a romantic relationship."

"Jesus," Zack breathed. "The girl is seventeen."

"I have no care for her age, only her importance."

There was a long pause as Zack studied the floor, his shoes, everything but the man sitting across the desk from him. "I … uh … I don't know how to say this. I appreciate everything you've done for me, hiring me and all. I recognize that this is a very good job, especially compared to what some of my classmates ended up with, but—"

"You are reluctant to infiltrate the confidences of a seventeen year old girl." Old Man Winter stared at him, knowingly.

"It doesn't seem right," Zack said. "She's—"

"She will be dead within a month unless she remains here," Old Man Winter said. "Or a captive of Wolfe, which will be no great kindness. Read his file. Watch the interrogation as Ariadne speaks with Sienna. I suspect you will see a defiant persona, one hesitant to trust. I ask you to act in her best interests, to keep her here and safe from harm."

Zack ran a hand through his hair, and the strands slipped through his fingers a few at a time. "I don't know. I mean … she's so young …"

"Of course, with this assignment," Old Man Winter said, "would come some additional benefits—a raise in pay, a promotion, the knowledge that your career with us is a very serious business for you. It would be an opportunity for you to prove yourself, to prove that you are capable of more complex assignments than simple … agent work."

I saw Zack swallow, his Adam's apple bobbing in his throat. "Yeah. Yeah, okay. It'd be like undercover work." I watched him go through a series of thoughts in his head, and I knew he was rationalizing something that he didn't really want to do. I'd seen the same look from him when I asked him to go with me to the mall. "That makes sense. And it's for her own good, after all. But uh … I mean, with a seventeen-year-old … I don't know that I feel comfortable with a romantic situation—"

"She is innocent," Old Man Winter said, his eyes slitting at Zack. "I doubt you will need to do much to gain her confidence other than show her some attention and perhaps some minor affection. Keep in mind that you will be the first person other than her mother to try and establish any connection with her."

"All right," Zack said, and his voice was a little stronger now. I could see the doubt percolating behind his eyes, but he nodded. "I can talk with her, try and ... sway her decision to stay, or at least try."

"Excellent," Old Man Winter said, cocking his head, blue eyes glaring with cold. "I had heard ... that you would be a reliable person in this matter. Someone we can ... count on."

The world of Old Man Winter's office faded, slipping away as surely as if I were falling through the floor. Everything went black around me, and I awoke with a sharp intake of breath, the cold air frosting in front of me. The temperature had dropped before I made it to the car, and by the time I had driven back to the farmhouse and raided Parks' stash of weapons it was well below freezing. I blinked the spots of light out of my eyes; I was still parked just outside the back door and the light was shining down on me. I took another breath, felt the cold air fill my nose and lungs, and realized that as I awakened, I could feel Zack recede to a dark place in the back of my head. I wanted to reach out to him, to bring him forward like the others, but I couldn't figure out how.

I lifted my head off the headrest and saw my new, pay-as-you-go cellphone sitting where I had left it in the cup holder below the front seat. I picked it up, watching the little blue LED indicator blinking to tell me I had a message. I thumbed it on and saw the time—four-thirty in the morning. I had been asleep for hours, and the chill had seeped in, and I realized that I felt it all the way through my aching body. I flipped to the message, which was a simple text, from Kurt:

Tomorrow. Nine AM.

He followed it with an address in St. Paul which was north of downtown, about a thirty-minute drive from my house. I cursed under my breath. I had an hour's drive just to get back home, and unless I wanted to go to bed covered in mud I'd have to shower. I'd be lucky to make it to bed before six a.m. I sighed and leaned my head against the headrest and shut my eyes again, just for a minute.

This one was for you, Zack, I thought. I felt the stir of the other three, but not him.

It was a very good job, Little Doll. A very good first step.

"Thanks for nothing." I fumbled and stuck the keys in the ignition, whilst trying to rub my hands enough to create some warmth. I eyed the light above Parks's door one last time as I shifted the car into drive. I ignored the groans of protest from the cold car as I turned around in the frozen driveway and headed up the dirt road back to the highway.

Seven

"He's gonna be a tough one," Kurt said, squinting his piggy eyes in the glare of the sunlight.

"Always has been," I said. I wore dark glasses, not only because of the sun shining overhead but because I didn't feel like having people look me in the eyes right now. "Why should it be any different when the time comes for him to die?"

There was a grunt of almost-amusement from the big man, and he nodded toward a building in the distance. The air was cold but not bitterly so. The sun had warmed it, and temperatures were back above freezing. We stood in a vacant lot, the ground soft beneath our feet as we stared at the ramshackle brick building across the street. It was a bar, an old one, and it looked as though it might fall down at any given moment. The decaying red brick looked as if it had been built a hundred years ago and repurposed into a bar in the last twenty or so. My eyes swept the street and found more of the same. The whole avenue was near-empty save a few parked cars, one of which was sitting on concrete blocks. In a parking space. Parallel parked. I shook my head at that, wondering if it had been the owner's choice and somehow doubting it. The whole place smelled of old diesel exhaust and oil, as if all the years of being near a major thoroughfare had left an olfactory mark on the neighborhood.

"Wanna go over it again?" Kurt asked, jamming his ham-like hands deeper into the pockets of his brown trench coat. A fedora was all that was missing to reinforce the illusion that he was a first-rate private eye from the thirties. I scanned the street again; the neighborhood was only helping that illusion.

"Simple enough," I said, throwing a hand out to point at the bar. "He's got a night off, he gets hammered in there, stumbles out around one a.m. if the pattern holds." I glared at the front door of the bar, which was red. "After that, it's all up to me."

"So, what are you gonna do?" Hannegan stared into the lenses of my glasses.

I felt a flash of annoyance but kept myself level. "Let me worry about that. What about the next one?"

He shook his head. "Eve's still in the Cities, but I'm having a harder time tracking her down because she's not hanging out with any of the guys. Same with Bastian. Not exactly buddy-buddy with Jackson or any of the others."

A cold wind whistled through, loud enough to blot out my hearing for a minute. "And Winter?"

"Working on it," Kurt said brusquely. "But trust me, you don't wanna even think about going after him until you thin out the M-Squad ranks a little more. Taking out Parks didn't really do you much good, though, since he wasn't even working for Winter anymore—"

"It did me worlds of good," I said, and stared at the front door of the bar, off in the distance. "Trust me." I held the glare on the bar. "One other thing."

"Hm?" Kurt had started to turn away, to head back to his car. "What?"

I licked my lips. "Did Zack ever say anything to you about Old Man Winter making him an offer when I first got to the Directorate?" I watched Hannegan's reaction; the big man froze in place, his whole frame stiffening. "Something about getting close to me in exchange for more money and a promotion?"

"I … uh …" Hannegan opened his mouth slightly, and turned his big body away from me to face the alleyway that we would have to walk back down to get to our cars. "He … might have mentioned something like that at the time, but I don't know that he went through with it."

"Then why are you cringing, Kurt?" I stared him down; he wouldn't have been able to see me flinch under the dark glasses I was wearing anyway.

"You know, he's dead," Hannegan said abruptly.

"I did notice that, yes," I said coldly.

"Might wanna just let that one lie." Hannegan looked back at me, stared me right in the sunglasses. "The man wasn't a saint, you know."

"That's interesting. He's as dead as one."

Hannegan took a deep breath. "I just meant … for what you're doing now, it might not bear a lot of deep scrutinizing about how the Directorate ran. You know what they did to him was meant for you, anyway, right? It had nothing to do with him. He was just …" Hannegan's voice trailed off, and a look of disgust cropped up over his blighted features, "… a human. Expendable. In the way."

"I know what they did," I said, looking back to the red door of the bar, "and I know how he felt, however we might have started." I said the words, trying to believe them down the core of me, "and I know what's going to happen when I meet Clyde Clary, when he stumbles out of that bar." I looked back across the deserted urban blight, only a few blocks away, as something I had seen on the satellite view of the map stood out to me. It was a crane, with its hook hanging high above the small buildings that dotted the landscape around me. "I know just what to do with … him." And I smiled.

Eight

The night was warmer, which fit well with my plans. The temperature was above freezing, but I still remained bundled in my coat as I lingered close to the alley entrance where Kurt and I had watched the bar. The chill had seeped in after a while, numbing my skin. I took a sniff and caught the smell of oil, though it was mixed with smoke from people who had stepped out of the bar for a quick cigarette before dodging back inside. Every time the red door opened, loud music echoed down the quiet street. A dog barked in the distance. I pulled my coat tighter. I could feel the anticipation in my mind—not mine, but that of the others.

When is the rock man going to come out, Little Doll?

"Why don't you try calling me something else for variety? Like Precious. I could hear you saying Precious and making it sound appropriately Gollum-y."

Wolfe senses that you're making fun of him, Little Doll.

"You have a good sense—in that area, at least." I peered at the red door, willing it to open, to discharge the one stupid soul I wanted to spill out onto the sidewalk. I hoped he was especially drunk tonight; it would make my job easier.

Not very nice, Little Doll.

"I remember when I used to be nice." I took a sniff of the cool air then almost snorted it out. "I think it ended the day I watched a psychopath squeeze the life out of a man in a parking lot while he choked the hell out of me."

Was that first time you saw death, Little Doll?

"It was." I blotted it out of my memory, the thought of that day. Two men had died, two young ones, in their twenties or so, just for trying to keep me from being killed. "It feels like I should remember them, remember their faces, but I can't. They died for me, the first of so many, and I can't even remember them."

It gets easier, the voice of Wolfe, dripping with sweet malice, came to me. *So much easier with time ... and practice.*

"You would know." I sucked in another breath, and the red door opened as though on cue. A bulky figure staggered out onto the broken pavement in front of the bar, a shoulder slumping as though he were ready to fall. He caught himself in time, steadying, before executing a sloppy turn to his left and taking a few staggering steps down the sidewalk. I felt myself smile, then let it disappear when I realized there was no joy behind it at all. "Showtime."

I crossed the street without fear; a car hadn't come by in the last hour I had been here, at least. Every step was heavy for me, and time was dragging slowly past. I kept focused on him, Clyde Clary, his bulk stumbling down the street with every sauntering step. He looked like an ape, shambling along, the missing link in the evolutionary chain. He had steadied himself a bit and was almost walking upright now—quite an accomplishment for him, I figured. I took in cold breaths of air, thankful once more that the temperature hovered above freezing. I stepped over a patch of brown grass as I mounted the curb and stepped onto the sidewalk behind him.

His steps were slow, shuffling, but when I was two feet behind him, he spun, faster than I would have thought possible in his present condition. "You picked the wrong guy to mug and on the wrong night," he said, throwing a hand out at me.

I backflipped into the air and landed ten feet from where I started. He stood there, staring, open-jawed, a blank look on his face as I landed delicately and stood straight up again. "What the?" His tone was dull, almost disbelief.

"Hello, Clyde," I said, still wearing my sunglasses. I was

wearing a shorter coat now, a leather one that reached only to my waist. Between it and the seething rage I was carrying, I felt like a little bit of a badass. "It's so good to see you."

He blinked at me, standing slack where he'd been when I approached him. His hands were at his side, and he was flat-footed. "What are you doing here?" He slurred his words and there was a tinge of innocence to his question, as if he was genuinely curious.

"Why, Clyde," I said, noting he didn't seem upset by my using his first name, "are you surprised to see me?"

"Well, yeah." The look on his face was so dull, I realized he hadn't come close to working out why I was here. Not yet, anyway.

"You shouldn't be." I cracked my knuckles and his eyes darted down to where my hands rested in front of me. I saw the slight widening of his eyes and I smiled in acknowledgment. "That's right," I said as I raised my bare hands up in front of my face. "The gloves are off, Clary."

He let out an almost weary sigh. "Girl, you know you can't hurt me with those." His head turned back toward me and in an eyeblink his skin had turned metal, as if liquid steel had been poured over him and conformed to every bump and scar on his bulky frame. "Just go on, now. Go on back home." He waved a hand at me like he was shooing off a wayward dog.

"I don't have a home anymore," I said, glaring him down behind my sunglasses. The lenses were tinted enough so that he couldn't see my eyes, but they were shaded in a way that I had no problem seeing everything around me. "Don't you remember? You took it from me." I slowly took my first step toward him.

He shook his head at me. "Girl—"

"My name isn't 'Girl'." My voice crackled with quiet fury down the abandoned street and Clary took a step back. "You'll remember that before we're finished."

"I know you who you are—"

"You have no idea who I am," I said, every word dripping with loathing, with frigid anger. "You don't know me."

"Just go on home and we'll forget this happened," he said with an air of growing desperation. "I don't want to have to kill you. Old Man Winter doesn't want you dead."

"Well, we wouldn't want to disappoint Old Man Winter," I said, taking a step forward.

"It ain't a wise idea to piss the old guy off," Clary agreed, watching me carefully.

"I know what Old Man Winter wants," I said, and took another step toward him. "I know what Winter wants better than you do."

"Well, he wants you not dead," Clary said, hesitating, "and if you keep coming at me, I'm gonna have to put you down, hard. You ain't got a prayer, girl. You can't even hurt me. Don't do it. Don't make me—"

I pulled my gun before he could say another word and snapped off three rounds. Two of the three plinked off his face; the third hit his left eyeball and drew a scream of pain. I felt an inadvertent grin split my lips. "You might want to reconsider that bit about me not being able to hurt you—"

He roared and came at me in a lunge. I saw a flash of red dripping down his cheek as he did it, his left eye a bloody, destroyed mess. I dodged left as he tore past me, the sidewalk cracking with every thunderous step he took. I bounced off the boarded-up brick storefront behind me as he passed and started to turn, looking for me with the one eye he had left.

"What's that old saying, Clyde?" I sneered at him as he came around to face me. "An eye for an eye?" He glared at me and I stared back at him, unruffled; my sunglasses were still unmoved.

"Oh, I'm gonna take more than an eye from you for that," he breathed.

"You already took more than that from me," I said, "and I mean to take more than that from you in return."

I raised the gun and fired again, but this time he was closer, close enough to raise a hand and block the shots with a ham-like palm. I tried to jerk my pistol away but his fingers closed on it entirely too quickly, and I heard the sound of the metal barrel creak as he bent it. I let it go and dodged to his left in a dead run, back toward the alleyway I had been standing in before.

"Where do you think you're going? " he shouted and I heard him take off after me, feet crashing against the pavement as he ran. I kept ahead of him, running at full speed through the alley. I dodged over the tripwire I'd left in the middle of it, hoping he wouldn't see it until it was too late—

The sound of a pallet of bricks falling onto Clary's metal head greeted my ears as he snagged the tripwire, followed by a sharp shout of rage. I tossed a look back over my shoulder when I heard them drop and watched as he disappeared under an avalanche of falling red bricks. I paused only a second, long enough to see him come out the other side of the cloud of dust where he had broken through them. I turned on the jets again, feeling my thighs pump up and down as I ran out the end of the alley and crossed the street beyond.

"DAMN YOU, GIRL!" The shout was like the end of the world, and was followed by the sound of a ton of metal leaping through the air behind me. Clary jumped twenty feet, surprising the hell out of me. I'd never seen him do anything like it before, and when he landed he did so not terribly far behind me. I jumped a chain-link fence in a single bound and heard him run through it behind me, the links snapping from the force of his charge. I landed in an overgrown field, my boots sinking into the mud from where the frost had melted but failed to be absorbed into the ground. The thick, sticky consistency of it caused me to waver for a moment before my feet broke free of the suction. I was moving again a second later, but it gave Clary a chance to close the gap between us to a little over five feet.

I was taking deep breaths by this point, the adrenaline pumping through my veins. I jumped the fence on the other side of the lot and landed on the sidewalk beyond. My eyes came up and fixed on my destination in the distance, not far now, only a couple of streets away—

I was still running when I felt something land on my coat collar. With a yank I felt myself ripped backward in a horse-collar tackle as my legs kept moving forward. The back of my neck was slammed into the street's hard asphalt. Pain ran down my spine from the impact and instantly my head pounded with searing agony. It felt as though someone had taken a spear and stabbed it through the top of my head and let it run down the base of my neck, shattering my spine all the way down. I heard a cry of pain, a gasp for air and I realized it was me.

A steel hand gripped me around the throat and tore me from the ground, lifting me into the air. He brought me up to his face, looked at me with his remaining eye, a singularly humorless expression etched on his metal features. "What were you saying about an eye for an eye, girl?"

"You owe me ... a hell of a lot more than your eyes." I ran a finger at him, straight on, with all my strength, pointed at the one good eye he had remaining. "But I'll take 'em anyway—" He caught my wrist with his other hand and I felt it snap, the sound of bones breaking in my forearm filling my ears along with a scream I hadn't meant to let go.

He levered me up and held my face against his bloody socket. "You are gonna pay for this, girl."

"You'd make a girl pay?" I asked, trying to breathe around the crushing pain of his hand squeezing me tight. "Explains why you don't date much."

"You always got a smart answer to everything, don't you?"

His metal head was nodding, slowly, his mouth a thin line of barely contained rage. "You think you're smarter than me. Better than me."

"Yes and yes," I said, squeezing in a breath. "But that's a low bar to clear. Kind of like the one you were just in, only seedier."

"You think you're better," he said again, looking at me with a calm self-satisfaction. "Miss High and Mighty. You ain't looking so high and mighty now, girl." He gripped my arm tighter and I heard the bones shatter completely; a scream tore loose from my throat as it felt like they turned to powders from the strength of his grip. "I've always been better than you. Always." He leaned in closer to me, and I could smell the whiskey fumes on his stinking breath. "I think it's time you realized that, too."

With that, he wound up, dragging my body behind him and then released me, throwing me overhand with all the effort of a pitcher sending a ball over the plate. I sailed through the air like a fastball, and when the strike out came it was me, crashing through the boarded up windows of a building across the street. I blacked out as I hit the concrete floor and came to rest, finally just as broken in body as I had felt in my mind.

Nine

My eyes blinked back open a moment later, and every single nerve in my body screamed at me. I took a hard breath, felt the sharpest sort of agony in my back, and tried to sit up. There were bones broken, I knew it—in my arm, my sides, maybe even my skull. The smell of refuse, the sharp odor of rotting garbage, was all around me and something else, like urine, stunk in the abandoned building. My eyes swept the darkness which filled the world around me. There was a faint flickering in the distance, and it took me a moment to realize it was coming through a roughly Sienna-sized hole in the plywood over the windows, my entry point to the building, where Clary had thrown me through the boards. It was only wide enough to admit a little of the light shining from the streetlights outside, which was blotted out a moment later by a face and broad shoulders as Clary peered in. He was shadowed, and I couldn't see anything but his outline, but I moved swiftly, rolling to the side as quietly as I could.

"Girl?" Clary's voice was unsure, as though there was some question about whether he had just thrown my limp body into the building. His hands came up and knocked away the remaining plywood, brightening the space around me by only a little. The lone streetlight outside wasn't doing Clary any favors, I realized as he started to step inside. Coming from the lit street into the darkness of the abandoned storefront meant his night vision was completely shot for a few seconds as his eye adjusted, and that was to my advantage. I looked behind me at the back wall of the space; I wasn't far away from where I wanted to be. Where I needed to be.

I brushed against a concrete block wall, now comfortably ensconced in the shadows of the empty storefront. I could see metal pillars that supported the roof, spaced every twenty feet or so. I wondered idly if I could ambush him somehow, maybe drop the roof on him or hit him with something from one of the refuse piles, but after a quick look around I dismissed both of those ideas. There was no sign of even a makeshift weapon anywhere in sight that would do any damage to Clary.

"Where you at?" His voice came again, but he was lingering toward the front of the store. I stayed still, now lying flat against the wall. Clary's remaining eye had to be nearly adjusted by now and motion would likely draw him to me. My eyes scanned past the pillars in the middle of the room. There were piles of rubbish every few feet, what looked like heaps of broken drywall and lumber, as though someone had demolished the interior of the space before vacating it but never bothered to clean it up. My eyes searched the walls; I had heard that scavengers had taken to stealing copper out of the fixtures of abandoned buildings but I couldn't see any pipes or fittings from where I lay.

"Come on out, now," Clary said, taking a tentative step forward. I tried to conjure a scenario in my mind where I ambushed him, grabbing him by his metal head and slinging him around like I had once done to another man who wore a skin of steel. That possibility fled even more quickly than the first idea; with a shattered arm, I doubted I'd be able to lift him. One arm was simply not enough to manhandle a beast like Clyde Clary, at least not in his metal form. "I'm not gonna hurt you." He seemed to realize the stupidity of this statement. "Well, I ain't gonna hurt you much." He paused. "More. Much more."

I looked at the back wall again, scanning for an exit, anything. It appeared to be solid concrete block back there, but surely there had to be a back door, something I could use to get outside, back on course, heading toward—

My eyes found it as I heard Clary take another step. This time his voice was cross. "Come on, now. I'm getting mighty sick of this!"

I kept my breathing low and steady. I tried to sit up but the pain was too much. I kept myself from doing much more than taking a sharp breath, but I heard Clary freeze.

"I hear you," Clary said, and I could sense the malicious glee behind the slurred words. "I'm gonna find you. It'll be easier if you just come out now."

Little Doll, Wolfe's voice came in my head, *run now.*

"I'd like to," I said, mumbling into my mouth without opening it, "but I don't think I can."

Go now, Little Doll.

There was a surge of something through me at the same time as I saw Clary's face turn toward me, his features still hidden in shadow. "Well … there you are."

I flung myself to my feet and ran, the pain receding as I did so. Clary let out a howl of outrage. "Where the hell do you think you're goin—"

I hit the exit door with my right shoulder, the one not attached to the shattered arm, and the frame splintered, throwing the door to the ground. The pain was gone, faded into the back of my head like a voice I could just barely hear. I turned right as I flew through the exit, sprinting on weary legs down another alleyway, this one asphalt. I reached the opening to the next street and heard Clary behind me coming out the door.

"You ain't gettin' away, girl!" I was in the street and almost across by the time he reached the mouth of the alley I had just left behind. The night was quiet save for his shouting and dogs barking in the distance. "I'll see you suffer for this!"

"I doubt you're gonna see much of anything with only one eye, Clyde." I took staggering steps across the sidewalk and into what appeared to be an empty construction site as Clary followed behind me. He didn't answer, but I heard him snort in rage behind me. I slowed my pace, taking careful steps on wooden planks that were lying atop canvas. Far above me, a gantry crane loomed, a giant corrugated metal cargo container in its grasp, dangling a hundred feet in the air directly over me.

"You can barely walk, girl," Clary said as I stopped and turned. He stood at the entry to the site, about thirty feet from me, the ground I had just trod the only thing separating us. I stared at him, my sunglasses gone, my face covered in blood, my entire body shaking from the brutal beating he had just given me. "You always thought you were too good," he said, his metal face leering with his missing eye puckered shut. "Betcha don't think that no more."

"You keep confusing bigger and stronger with better," I said, my voice consumed with utter loathing. I snorted, letting my nostrils flare. "It isn't. There's a world of difference between being bigger than someone and being better than someone. And you? You've always been a waste of human flesh. A disgusting pig with no regard for anyone but himself, so ugly on the inside that the only thing that beats it is how ugly you are on the outside." I sneered at him and saw his face darken. "I've always been better than you, because I'm smarter than you. And you've always been too stupid to realize it."

He face crumpled in pure fury, his eyebrows perfectly downturned and his lips a jagged line. "I'm 'bout to beat that superiority right outta you, bitch—" He took a heavy step toward me, a long one, long enough to carry him to me in about four good strides. It was perfect, really, just enough fury to carry him on. The first step he landed on the same piece of lumber I had walked on, and it made a straining crack as he did it. Lucky, I thought. His next step was not so fortunate.

He came down with his right foot, all his weight on it as he prepared to charge at me, to smear my smug, taunting face all over the construction site we were standing in. He landed on the canvas that covered the ground rather than the boards that I had been walking on, though, and his remaining eye widened as he disappeared through the ground, falling through the trap I had laid for him. The board I had walked on followed after him, along with the canvas that covered over the new public swimming pool that the citizens of St. Paul had commissioned to be built in the summer, the one that hadn't opened yet, and that the construction company hadn't bothered to move their equipment out of yet. Times were tight, after all, and with winter coming it hadn't been likely that they'd get another contract to build something before spring thawed the earth. Which was why they locked all their tools and supplies up in the corrugated metal container and hoisted it a hundred feet up in the air with the crane. No one was going to steal a crane, after all, even if they knew how to use it—which I didn't.

I took limping steps over to a rope I had tied to the release for the cargo container. I didn't know how to use a crane, but I knew how to pull a lever, and I'd attached a rope to it earlier that day expressly for that purpose. Doubtless whoever had secured it hadn't considered the possibility of a girl with my athletic prowess coming along to drop it.

I heard stirrings in the empty pool below, the sound of angry grunts as Clary righted himself and ripped his way through the canvas tarp that had hidden the pool from his sight. "Dammit, girl, I am gonna skin your ass alive now, that and the whole rest of you, too. I'm gonna lay a whooping on you so hard that you're gonna wish your ass had been trampled to death by a herd of cows, because it'd be faster and sweeter. Old Man Winter said not to kill you, but dammit, I'm gonna do everything short of it—" His head appeared above the lip of the pool and I tossed him a cordial wave with my broken arm as I pulled hard on the rope with the other. There was a subtle groan a hundred feet above us and Clary looked straight up. I could imagine his remaining eye widenening as it came down on him, but he didn't move, not nearly in time.

I had estimated, when I had been up on the rig earlier to attach the rope, that the container weighed at least a couple tons. It was laden with all manner of machinery, and when it hit Clary it made a loud noise, about what you'd expect from tons of metal hitting a man-pig-sized object also made of metal. The force and sound of the impact was something that would have set off the car alarms all around if there had been any. A cloud of dust swept over me from the impact as I eased up to the edge of the pool. The cargo container had caught Clary perfectly; he was pinned beneath it, both arms trapped under his body. The beam of it ran over his shoulders, arched from landing on him, bent from hitting the immovable object that was Clyde Clary.

"Girl ..." Clary said, and his voice was low and menacing, "you are gonna PAY for this."

"You keep saying that," I replied and took a slow walk around the edge of the pool. His head swiveled to follow my progress as I walked toward the small hut that housed the mechanical equipment to keep the pool clean. "And I'll admit, you did a hell of a number on me, Clyde." I paused. "But that's the last time you'll ever lay so much as a fingertip on me."

"Oh, I'll take that bet. You know this ain't gonna keep me down forever," he grumbled, and I saw him strain to lift it. It moved, but only subtly, and he stopped. "Just a matter of time before I work my way outta this, and I will find you. And I will HURT you. Worse than you have ever been hurt before in your entire mean-girl life."

"No, Clary," I said, resting my hand on the long handle of a wrench I'd left attached to the fire hose spigot built into the side of the mechanical hut. I assumed it was required by zoning regulations because it didn't make an overabundance of sense to me why a fire hose would ever be needed on a pool, but since it

worked to my advantage I didn't intend to complain. "You won't."
I turned the wrench and opened the spigot. The water surged on,
spraying past me to the edge of the pool, drenching the sidewalk
and running over the edge. "You've just about oinked your last."

The spray was blasting now, the loudness of the surging water
drowned out his next response. I walked back around the edge,
closer to where he lay in the deep end of the pool. Water was
beginning to collect now, running toward him, starting to gather
around him. His face was wet from it, just a little bit thus far, and I
saw the eye calculating as he strained against the container that
had him pinned. "This ain't funny, girl."

"No," I agreed. "It's not."

He pushed against it again, as the water climbed another few
centimeters to reach his chin. He spit as he tried to breathe, a spray
of water shooting from his mouth and misting in the air. "Come
on." I watched him, unfeeling as he struggled against the tons of
weight on his shoulders. "Ha ha ha. This is a good one, I gotta
admit!" he shouted. "You got me! You got me good!" I didn't
answer, just kept staring at him, and the first sign of nerves
appeared on his metal face. "Come on now, girl—"

"My name is Sienna."

He looked at me in near-astonishment, the full gravity of what
was happening starting to dawn on him. "Come on, now, Sienna!
You can't leave me like this!"

"Leave?" I kept staring. "Why would I leave? I've got the
best seat in the house."

He stared at me in dull disbelief as the water covered his
mouth and he forced it above the roiling surface of the water.
"Sienna! Sienna!" His face lowered into the water again for a few
seconds, and then he pushed the container up enough to get his
mouth above water one last time. "For the love of—!" With that,
his mouth went under, and he struggled to keep his nose above the
rising water.

"I think the line you're looking for is, 'For the love of God, Montresor!'" I watched as he took a deep breath, watched the water rise above his eyes, and he continued to struggle against the weight that trapped him. The container moved a little, here and there, as Clyde Clary fought against it. He jerked left and right, up and down, for almost two minutes as the hose continued to spit his death upon him until finally he stopped moving. There was a ripple under the surface and I watched his steel skin turn again to pink flesh as Clyde drowned. With the creaking of shifting metal, the container settled on him and blood bubbled up to the surface, turning the water as red as the rage that still fed my soul.

Ten

The world was a bending, twisting mass around me. I knew I was sleeping, and I had the presence of mind to realize I was dreaming. It was getting a little easier to discern these dreams. You would think, since one of my powers is to reach out to others in their dreams, that I'd know my own when I saw them. These were so strange, though, so unrelated to dreaming, that I didn't.

There was a heavy smell of cologne in the air, overpowering, enough that it made me want to cough, even in the insubstantial form I was in. There was a mirror in front of me, and I could see Zack in it, the whole world around me a purplish haze from neon lighting. It was a bar, the one I'd met Kurt in just a few days earlier. I shook my non-existent head to clear some of the fog, but failed; the world around me remained shrouded in a haze. I looked right and saw Zack sitting next to me, an amber beer filling the tall mug he had in front of him. He picked it up and took a sip, and I could smell it like I was drinking it myself, the sour scent hanging in my nose.

"You don't look happy." Kurt's voice was audible over the music but just barely. I looked out onto the dance floor, and there were actually a decent number of people dancing. A DJ was waving his hand in the air as he spun his records and a crowd of dancers filled the floor. I noted they were mostly women. They all seemed older, I realized. Past their twenties, for certain. There were a half dozen of them on the dance floor, all dolled up, clearly drunk. I turned back to where Zack and Kurt sat at the bar, and tried to listen to the big man speak to my dead boyfriend.

"I'm fine," Zack said, taking another sip and overpowering

me with the aroma of beer as he finished the glass.

"Your alcohol disagrees with you, lightweight." Kurt gave him a cocked eyebrow then a shrug before he went back to his own glass. The stool Kurt was on looked like it was bending under his weight, but it might have been my imagination.

"Okay," Zack said, and halted as he waved to the barman for another round. "Okay, so …" He paused, and I could see on his face a look that was the same as when he struggled to tell me something. I felt a pang; I always thought it was cute.

Hannegan didn't. "Spit it out already, will you?" The older man scowled. "Lemme guess … girlfriend problems?"

"Yes," Zack said as a new beer was set before him. "Kind of."

Hannegan shook his head and took a sip. "She's damaged goods, man. Take her back and exchange her for store credit." He turned his head around to look at the dance floor. There was a woman on the edge of the crowd, trying to pretend she wasn't looking right at Zack. "Maybe get something in blond instead."

Zack kept facing the bar, eyes down, unaware of anything around him. I could see the look, like he was in his own head, trying to root things out. "I just … I mean, she's in training right now, okay? For M-Squad, and I think—"

"Man," Kurt said, turning back to him. "There is a cougar out there on the dance floor who is hot for you."

"What?" Zack said, blinking, staring at Hannegan in confusion. "I'm talking about Sienna here, okay? Try not to distract me."

"Right," Kurt said. "You're talking about the girlfriend you can't touch." He cast another look back to the dance floor. "I thought you were just with her because of Old Man Winter's orders?"

Zack froze, his mouth slightly open. "You know about that?"

"Oh, yeah," Kurt said, turning back. "You told me yourself,

before you went down to South America to retrieve M-Squad a couple months ago." He set his beer back down on the bar. "Not surprised you don't remember; you were pretty drunk when you told me. All emotional and guilty." He took a deep sniff and turned back to the bar. "I honestly felt bad for you. Being told you have to date a girl to keep your job ... it's kinda like if your boss was holding it over your head to take a girl to prom because she's his daughter. But for you ... even worse. Not only is your girl a broken piece of a human being—I mean, locked in a tin can in the basement by her mother after being imprisoned for a decade with no one to talk to but a mommy who doesn't love her?" Kurt snorted. "She's a special kind of damaged. But to have to pretend to be her boyfriend AND know that you're never going to get laid because it'll kill you?" He let out a bellowing laugh. "It's like icing on a crap cake. Poop frosting." He leaned closer to Zack. "Tell me it doesn't weigh on you."

Zack seemed a little flushed; I could see that the alcohol was taking effect, even as he took another long pull from his beer. "Yeah. I mean, yeah, hell yeah, it does." He tossed a look back to the dance floor and locked eyes with the cougar; she was blond, and hot, willowy where I wasn't, wearing tons of makeup and doing a pretty great job of hiding her age, at least in the darkness of the bar.

Kurt leaned in closer to him and nodded to the blond in the distance. "You know ... I bet you could have her." He slapped a meaty paw on Zack's shoulder. The blond gave Zack a come-hither sign with her finger that was about as subtle as a kick to the groin. Which I would have delivered to him myself had I really been there at that moment. "A real girl. You could touch her and everything—"

"I know what I can do," Zack said, turning away, back to the bar, and taking a long drink from his beer.

"That's the spirit, kid," Kurt said, "liquid courage."

"Yeah," Zack said, and he stood. "It's not like … I mean, it's not like I'm cheating on Sienna, is it?"

Kurt blew the air out through his lips in utter disbelief. "Aren't you getting paid to go out with her?"

Zack's eyes darted up, as though he were thinking about it. "Technically, yes, but—"

"Then it's not cheating because she's not your real girlfriend." Kurt's voice of authority sent ripples of outrage through me. I was stuck, though, frozen here in the dream state, watching this all unfold. "Have a good night, champ. You've earned it."

"Yeah," Zack said quietly as he stood, straightening his suit coat and checking the first button on his shirt; it was down just a little, the way I liked it. He took a slow, ambling walk toward the dance floor and the blond that waited for him.

It was like being stuck watching a TV that you desperately wished you could turn the channel or look away from. I couldn't, though, couldn't even close my eyes. I watched, watched as they danced, hands fumbling in all the wrong places, drunken, watched her kiss him, then again, and again, as the music turned slow. I wanted to scream but there was no sound as time moved on and I was forced to follow them back to his apartment, making out in the back of a cab all the while, and then the stumbling walk up his stairs—

—I'd made that walk with him before, but neither of us were stumbling—

—They were kissing, deep, passionate, excited—

—The way I'd never been able to with him for fear of his life—

And when they were inside, clothing was shed, and she halted, just for a second, her age showing in the crinkling of the crow's feet around her eyes. Her voice was throaty as she broke away from kissing down his neck and chest. "You don't have a girlfriend or anything, do you?" Zack paused, opened his eyes and looked down at her, and his mouth opened, but nothing came out. "I mean, I don't care if you do—" she said and went back to kissing him just below the collarbone.

"No," he breathed at last, and she came up to lock lips with him. "I don't have a girlfriend," he said as they broke apart, and he ran his hands down her bare back, skin to skin. I watched them collapse onto the bed, in each other's arms, watched them intimate in a way I had only been with him once, and closer than I had been able to achieve without hurting him seriously—

—so many kisses, so much touch, his flesh to hers, no barriers between them—

I wanted to be nauseous, I wanted to be murderous, I wanted to intervene, to hit them both, to destroy the room around them, but I couldn't. I stood there, watching, as ephemeral as the air, as they made love, slowly, passionately, her cries of pleasure echoing in my ears and giving voice to the scream of agony that wanted to claw its way out of the throat I didn't presently have.

Eleven

I awoke in my own bed, a ragged scream on my lips that I killed as surely as I'd killed Parks and Clary. I fought for even breaths, slow, stable ones that didn't have me gasping as I sat there. My bed stunk of sweat, as though I'd gotten in it after my fight with Clary instead of waiting until after I'd showered (which I had). I looked at the wrist that he'd broken and it pulsed instead of throbbed. All my pains had become aches in the aftermath of the fight, well on the way to being back to normal. Light streamed in through the curtains at the sides where there was a gap between them and the wall. I'd moved the armoire that used to block the window after I'd started making the house payments with my Directorate salary.

The sheets were wet around me with the sticky sweat of my skin, alive with the smell of that dampness, and I looked over the remains of my room. Other than changing the positions of the furniture so I could see out the window, all my stuff was still mostly where it had been. My minimal personal belongings.

The last remnants of my sheltered life.

The bookshelf was filled to the brimming with books, all the volumes I'd spent my time with when I wasn't learning the basic skills mother expected me to pick up. There were novels, hundreds of them, all the books on which I'd based my outlook on the world when I wasn't pulling it from the hour of TV I was allowed to watch every day. I got out of bed and wandered idly over, paging through the spines as I ran my index finger over them. Fantasy, romances, science fiction; I'd read them all. Mother used to bring home a crate of used books every month or two, and I'd go through them, reading them one by one. I'd have to give up a crate to get another, though, because she always claimed we hadn't enough space to simply keep acquiring them. Once my shelf was full, I had to start cutting the ones I wanted to keep, until finally I had a shelf so filled with my favorites that every choice I made to give one up was as painful as saying goodbye to a dear friend. Every book I got rid of in order to add a new classic was a sacrifice. It had been the only way I'd felt emotions, other than through TV. It was the only way I'd felt connected to people. I was a mimic, and I tried to match how to feel with the way people felt in the stories I read and watched. I wondered how well it had translated.

Seeing the memories from Zack's unguarded moments told me that it had not translated well at all. I'd been a freak from the beginning, ill-equipped to do anything but snarl at the people around me at the Directorate. I swallowed and felt that lump in my throat again. He hadn't ever really been 'into' me. He was paid to feign interest by Old Man Winter.

I felt the burn of bile in the back of my throat.

That's right, Little Doll. Now you see how the old frost giant pushed you all along, manipulated you, played games with you.

"You're about as helpful as a paddle made of papier-mache, aren't you?" I sighed and closed my eyes.

He played with the Little Doll, with her emotions—

Yes, Bjorn agreed, *this is the way of Erich Winter, and has been for as long as I have known him, all the way back to—*

"I get it, you're all old, you've known each other since thousands of years ago. Congrats on being part of the world's first gentleman's club—you know, absent any actual gentlemen. And honestly, probably absent any of the other things you'd find in a more modern gentleman's club, like—"

Please, came Gavrikov's voice, *I must know more about my sister—*

"Oh, shut up about your sister already," I said, and Bjorn and Wolfe chorused their agreement. "No one cares about Kat, or whatever her name was before she evacuated her brain." I felt the burn of anger. "She'll be lucky if I don't test Charlie's advice about finding out what a Persephone's soul tastes like when next she crosses my path." My skin burned and I felt a strange desire to act out my words. "I wonder if she'd be all peppy like Kat if I drank her up or if she'd be like the slutty, grave-robbing whore that she is now—"

There was a flare in my head that felt like pain, like someone lit a pole on fire and thrust it into my ears, and it felt like fire burned, flashing around me as I fell to the floor. I gasped at the agony in my head, and only managed to open my eyes again after I felt Bjorn, Wolfe and another presence in my mind somehow battering Gavrikov to the back of my head, where he could do no harm. I lay on my bedroom floor, staring at the ceiling, as the thought of flame receded to the back of my consciousness. I could almost smell smoke somewhere in the distance.

Are you all right, Little Doll?

"Stop frigging calling me that," I said, massaging my forehead with my thumbs. "I have a name." There was a pause, silence, and I sat up. I clenched my eyes shut and let the hammering in my temples subside. There was a beep somewhere in the background and my eyes opened just wide enough to realize what it was. I crawled my way to the bed and reached up on the bedside table. The phone's screen flared to life at the press of a button and I saw I had a new text message.

Downtown, the Carver Building. #2883. Will be there tonight after 7 p.m.

I read it twice, just to be sure, then turned off power to the phone. "Thanks, Kurt," I whispered to myself.

You've done so well thus far, Little Doll—

"I told you to stop calling me that."

—such fine work, what you've done. With the metal man especially, such a tasty way to beat him. Wolfe could not have planned it better himself—

Very well thought out, I heard a grudging respect in Bjorn's tone, and it made me hate myself. *Killing a stoneskin is not easy, not even for a succubus.*

"I don't know what I'm doing anymore," I said and let the weariness settle over me. I saw Parks' face in my mind, after I'd shot him, how deformed and destroyed it was after I'd sent bullet after bullet through it, the gray hair and beard drenched with blood and flecked with tissue. I envisioned Clary, and felt a stir within as Wolfe trilled with pleasure and I tingled with disgust. All I could see in the water was red, blood floating in wisps like threads weaving their way through it in the dark of the streetlamps; it was more black than anything, but my mind painted it the way I knew it was, crimson, violent, horrible. Just like what I'd done to them.

"Zack never loved me," I whispered. "He was just doing what Old Man Winter told him to do."

All the more reason to make Winter pay, Wolfe said. *The Little Doll was hurt by him and hurts even worse now. Jotun must have known that the Little Doll would find this out; he rubs your face in his cruelty, taunts you with it, as if to show her that no one has ever cared for her. Winter orchestrated a great show to fool her, to play with her, to make her do his bidding ...*

Even at our height, with the most ruthless Primus at the head, Omega would not be so vicious, Bjorn said, and I could almost see his smile of self-satisfaction. *Killing is not cruel compared to what he has done to you. A beating is physical; it fades in time. We are metas, we do not scar like ordinaries—like humans do. But this, what he has done ... this will leave marks. He tries to make you more like him—*

"More like all of you," I said, and I knew it was true. "He wants me to kill."

But surely he can't think the Little Doll can kill him, Wolfe said.

"He thinks I'll try."

But he thinks the doll will fail, Wolfe hissed, *and that makes him a fool. Little Doll is stronger than Winter realizes.* I felt the burn in my guts, like ground glass was moving inside me, shredding my insides, then I felt it stop as though it had come up against a wall of concrete. *Little Doll will show him; she won't stop. Jotun probably thought the Little Doll would fail by coming at him with all his bodyguards around to save him. She won't, she'll remove them one by one until it's just him and her, and then we'll show her how to strip the frozen meat from his bones, oh yes, we will—*

There was a cry inside me, a howl of pure emotion whose source I knew. "Shut up, Zack," I said. "You don't even have the guts to speak to me, you just keep letting your sad and guilty memories float to the surface of my mind while I sleep." I grabbed the bed and used it to pull myself up. "I don't need your advice anymore. I'm not doing this for you, not now." I pictured them in my head, M-Squad and Winter. The two of them that were dead and the three I had left to go. I lifted my cell phone and stared at the blank screen. "It's for me, now. I'm doing this all for me." I looked toward the window, the barest hint of light creeping from behind the curtains, letting me know it was day outside, even though the room remained in shadow. "And I don't really care what happens after I'm finished."

Twelve

The cold night air was agonizing as I pushed open the heavy glass and metal door with a click and made my way into the residential apartments. The security man rose to greet me with a smile as I came in, the autumn-winter air stuck in my nose. It was below freezing again, not that I cared. I huddled within my coat less for warmth than to conceal what I was carrying beneath it. The first whiff of the building's heating system was sweet, a new smell for a new building.

The lobby was all sleek lines and classic styling; it reminded me of a photo I'd seen of a hotel lobby in Vegas. Behind the desk the security guard smiled and I feigned one back as I approached his desk. The sidewalks were empty at this time of night, especially on a weeknight.

"Cold out there?" he asked, with a knowing smile.

"It's cold everywhere," I replied, letting mine fade as I reached the front of the desk. "Hi. I'm Sienna." I stuck out my bare hand as though for him to shake it.

He looked at me curiously for a moment before grasping my outstretched hand and giving it a shake. "Nice to meet you, Sienna. I'm gonna need to see your I.D. to let you through, or else call the apartment you're going to in order to get their approval to send you up."

"Nah," I said, and held onto his hand. His palm was warm, his dark skin contrasted against my snow-pale hands. "I'm just here to introduce myself. I wouldn't want you to go waking anybody up." I gently pumped his hand, as though I'd forgotten I was shaking it.

He drew his eyes down, and gave me a faint look as though I

were crazy. "Well, Miss—"

"Sienna," I corrected him.

"Sienna," he said, and the first notes of him humoring me crept into his tone, "as nice as you are, if you're not here to see someone, I'm afraid I'm gonna have to ask you to move along." He tried to pull his hand away but failed as I held it tighter.

I pretended to think about it as he made another effort to get his hand free of mine and failed. His eyes widened and I knew the first stirrings of pain would be hitting him right about now. "I don't think so," I said and eyed his nametag, "Phil. Phil's a nice name." I held his hand tight, and he made a serious effort to pull away and failed, his eyes growing large in desperation. They were brown, like Zack's. "Listen, Phil," I pulled his arm, and he grunted in surprise as I yanked him forward, over the desk. I heard his knees hit the edge on his side and I knew he'd be feeling it in the morning, "I told you, I don't want you to wake anyone up. I am here to see someone, someone who doesn't want to see me, and I just … don't need any attention. Phil's eyes were wide, now, and I brought my other hand down to his cheek and stroked it with a sort of reassurance I didn't feel at all, even as he was squealing. I ignored every sound that came out of him as his eyes fluttered in pain.

Yes, Little Doll, like that—

"I don't need any help right now, thanks," I muttered as Phil looked at me one last time before his eyes rolled to unconsciousness. I held my contact with his skin for only a moment more before letting him go, and his body sagged, half-stretched over the desk. I gripped his shirt as I walked around and slid him back into his chair, letting him rest in a sleeping position, head leaned back. "I've got this."

Of course, Little Doll.

I felt the seething at that and knew he was pushing me, trying to make me angry before what was about to happen. "I don't need your help getting pissed off at these people, Wolfe."

But the Little Doll works so much better when she is angry. It's almost like art, and anger is the flavor, the expression. Wolfe's best works always had some sort of emotion put into them—tragedy, pathos, terror—

"Please don't recount your greatest hits right now," I said, and strolled back to the elevator, "unless you want me to go from angry to nauseous." I pushed the button for the twenty-eighth floor and then hit the elevator's close button.

Oh, of course. This reminds Wolfe, though, of a time in London, not long before he came to Minneapolis and met the Little Doll—

"Before I killed you, you mean?" I felt a self-satisfied smile creep on my face.

Killed the Wolfe, oh yes, the Little Doll did. But the Wolfe made a glorious show of it before he went, made many, many people go before him, made much art in the days before he went out. There was a little smile in his voice, too, that I could hear in my head. The low sound of the elevator ascending was background noise for the maniac in my head telling me about his finest hour. *To go out after a full life of work such as that, well … it is all that Wolfe could have hoped for and more.*

The elevator dinged. "And here I thought that Wolfe would have aimed to keep living and keep killing," I said acidly. "But no, all this time you were just looking for a way to leave a legacy of carnage that will only be dimly remembered given time."

Little Doll teases, but Wolfe isn't dead, not so long as the Little Doll remembers him, keeps him safe inside her—

"Ugh," I said. "Enough." I unbuttoned my coat and let it fall in the hallway. I pulled the H&K MP5K submachine gun that I wore on a strap across my midsection into my hand. It was the same weapon I had been trained with, and something that I'd pulled from Parks' basement along with four pistols I had holstered on my hips and under my arms. "Time to kill a faerie."

I paused outside the door of number 2883 for only as long as it took to check to make sure I had a bullet chambered. A moment later I kicked down the door with a crash and burst through. The smell of something spicy, like peanut noodles, hit me as I threw myself into the room. It was a kitchen and living room, barely lit, and all it took was a quick sweep with my eyes to see that the finely appointed but sparsely furnished space was empty. Bookshelves lined the wall to my left. I heard movement beyond a door in the middle of them and I ran for it, sweeping into a bedroom in time to see two figures in motion coming out of the bed. One was already on her feet, the other was going more slowly at half speed, struggling to get free of the sheets. I smiled predatorily as I raised my weapon at the target on the left side of the bed.

Eve Kappler was standing there, naked, her chiseled muscles and flawless skin making her look positively statuesque as she threw a hand up at me. I pulled the trigger and felt a three-shot burst echo through the room and lit the entire place in a flash of the muzzle. By the light of the flashes I saw the bullets impact, and her flat belly distended as the first shot hit her on the left side, the second in her ribcage under her left breast and the third presumably missed. The muzzle flash went off again as her net of light energy caught me, pulling my gun up and against my chest, causing me to pull the trigger again. Another three-shot burst went off, this time stitching the ceiling and walls as the net carried me back and slammed my back into the counter as the web knitted itself to the first surface it came across, the island in the center of the kitchen.

I felt my ribs break in my lower back as I hit, and the jolt caused me to fire again, the bullets shredding the light-based filaments of the net and forcing the barrel to poke out of where it had torn through the web that had me restrained. I tried to ignore the searing pain in my back; I was bent at an almost L-shaped angle backward, my lower torso and abdomen cemented to the kitchen island, the granite countertop anchoring part of my upper body where the net had caught me from just below the collarbone all the way to mid-thigh. I strained and felt it give at the weak point where the gun barrel had slid through, so I tried to force my weapon into the tear. I felt it rip a little at a time there but give very little on the hold it had around the rest of my body.

"Well, well," I heard a strained voice from the bedroom door. Eve staggered out, still nude, blood running down her side where I'd shot her. "It turns out the little kitten has some claws after all. I wouldn't have predicted it, no matter what Winter said." Her thick German accent was tinged with a rasp, and I suspected the shot I'd landed in her ribs had punched through her lung. She leaned against the frame, her hand holding tight and smearing the white trim with a bloody palm print as she used it to hold herself up. Red dripped down from the wound on her front; I was sure that my first shot had popped her in the kidney, and it pumped a little crimson out with each beat of her heart.

"Not a kitten," I said through gritted teeth and tried to angle the barrel toward her, standing in front of the open door. It was about twenty degrees off, I reckoned, and her webbing wasn't tearing very quickly. I could almost feel it ripping strand by strand, but the glow told me there were thousands of strands, and it reminded me of the time I saw Kat slowly sawing through her old denim jeans with a pocket knife, trying to turn them into cutoffs. "And just as an aside, I've got a hell of a lot more than claws. I've got things you wish you had," I said, stalling for time as she eased off the doorframe, the ambient light from the city skyline casting her still-naked body in stark relief. "I've guns. I've got bad attitude, and … um … clothing."

"I don't need any of those things." She said it with such self-assurance that I knew she wasn't kidding.

"Are you sure? You look like you could at least use a bra."

"You think you can shoot your way into my home, then talk your way out of it when things go badly for you?" Eve asked, taunting. I could see the blood that had been pumping out of the hole in her side was oozing more slowly. I looked closer and realized her skin was glowing; she had looked like she was stroking herself but she'd really been using her light webs to patch her own wounds. "I suspect Winter would like to talk to you. Though I'm inclined to make you hurt for a while before I bring you to him. And I think you'll need to be declawed first, kitten."

"Winter wants to talk to me?" I kept sawing for all I was worth as Eve began to circle wide around me to the right, well out of the arc of my gun. "That's good. I have a few choice things I'd love to say to him as well."

"Maybe you misunderstand," Eve said, easing closer to me, leaning over me from the safe side to approach. The filaments ripped, and it felt like I had torn through into a weaker section of the web. My arm moved now as well, my right one, and I felt it under the net as it broke free and I regained some mobility. "He isn't going to be interested in a single dull-witted thing you have to say," she reached a hand up and condescendingly gave me a gentle pat on the cheek, "he's going to talk, and you'll listen." She put her hand above my face, palm out, and I knew what she was going to do before she even started to do it. "But you're unlikely to shut up, so I'll just help him with that—"

With a last tug I felt my right hand tear free; the gun, unfortunately, did not follow, and before Eve could cover my mouth with her light web, I reached out and stabbed a finger into the bullet wound I'd left in her abdomen. She shrieked and doubled over, and I felt the strength of the webs loosen as she slapped a hand on my arm with enough force to break it had I been as slow as a normal human. I moved it in time and threw my forearm against her neck, pulling her around into a chokehold as I tried to get the rest of my body free, her back pressed against my front.

She bucked in pain, and I could tell the screaming agony I had caused in her abdomen was the only thing keeping her from throwing her head back hard enough to break my face. I tried to wrestle her struggling body with one arm while she fought me. When she dodged to my left, I tried to get my left hand up to the trigger of my submachine gun to put a few more holes in her, but it was still firmly anchored to the front grip by the light web.

She wrenched free with a gasp of pain and I lifted my booted foot and kicked her in the bare ass, sending her tumbling to the ground. As she landed, I felt the web that was pinning me to the island weaken further and I tore loose, watching the threads of light disintegrate as I ripped free and stood under my own power. I pulled the nearest convenient pistol to my dominant hand, the one on my right hip, and started shooting as I came up. Eve looked back in time to see me before I could fire and rolled to her left, her wings sprouting in the dark as she did so, though I couldn't hear them flutter over the sound of the gunshots. I tracked along her path and hit her again as she came to her feet, a solid shot to the shoulder with a .45. She staggered, now halfway across the living room. I pumped another round into her back, hitting her low, between her spine and hip on her right side.

Her arms pinwheeled as she hit the glass windows on the far side of the living room. I advanced on her without fear now, her hands smearing bloody streaks on the glass as she used it to keep herself from falling. I shot her again, this time in the right thigh, and I saw the glass crack as the bullet traversed her body and went out the other side. She fell hard against the window, causing a spider web of cracks to spread from where the bullet had torn through it, and she forced herself to turn to face me. Blood oozed out of her mouth, down her pale chin, and I could see every single wound I had put in her, the agony writ on her expression. She clenched teeth outlined in blood as she lay there against the window, half-turned to face me.

"Looks like … I was wrong … about you …" she said, and a bubble of blood formed on her lips as she spoke. "You're not … as weak as I thought you were. You always … hesitated before … at what needed to be done."

I shot her again, this time through the left shoulder, and she screamed, though I couldn't really hear it as the sound of the shot subsided. "I got over that after I shot Parks in the face a few times and drowned Clary."

She took halting breaths, and I saw fear mixed with admiration creep over her face as the cracks in the window worsened as her weight was pushed against them. "You killed Clary? And Parks?" Her accent was thicker now, her words slurred. "I wouldn't have thought … you could …"

"You should leave the thinking to someone more capable of it," I said, keeping my distance but shifting my aim. "But after my next shot that's not gonna be a problem for you anymore." I lined up the sights with her forehead. "Where is Old Man Winter?"

"I …" She choked on blood. It ran down her chin and fell over her chest, making for a grisly sight when coupled with the wounds elsewhere on her body. She looked worse than James Fries did after she had beat him into a pulp. "I … wouldn't tell you. You're going to kill me anyway."

"Yep," I said. I adjusted my aim and shot her in the kneecap, causing her to squeal in pain. "But how much it hurts before I do is entirely your prerogative."

"Torture?" She said with something between a laugh and a cry. "I didn't think you had the stomach for it."

"Times change," I said. "Amazing how motivated I got to learn new skills after you and your best pals murdered my boyfriend."

"He never cared for you," she said with a straight face. She looked me straight in the eyes with those cold blues of hers. "He was—"

"I know what he was," I said, and started to aim my gun again, this time at her other shoulder. "And I know what you and yours did. And I know what I'm going to do now. How much do you want to hurt before you die, Eve?"

She looked at me with a defiant gaze, holding her lip from quivering. "You can't hurt me enough to make me tell you what you want to know."

Kill her, Wolfe suggested with some glee, out of nowhere, *she will never talk.*

I nodded slowly. "You're probably right. Let's just get this over, with, shall we?" I pointed the gun back to her head, watched the defiance slip from her face as I tightened my finger on the trigger—

Something hit me in the head, something heavy, and my aim was thrown off just enough. I fired, and saw the bullet go through Eve's shoulder and shatter the glass behind her. The blond woman's weight carried her out, and I saw her fall for only a moment before her wings shone in the light and caught her, and she fluttered off. I fired the rest of my magazine at her and felt something else hit me in the side of the head. It smarted, and I saw it as it fell out the window, a simple, leather-bound hardback book. I turned and aimed my pistol at the figure standing there before me.

Her red hair danced in the cold wind that blew through the apartment now that the glass window was completely shattered and blown out. She held her blue silken bathrobe closed with her hands as she stood awkwardly, exposed, by the bookshelf near the bedroom door. I took a step closer to her, my gun obviously emptied of all bullets, the slide cocked back to expose the bare chamber. "Hello, Ariadne."

"Sienna," she said, and her left hand went to the bookcase for another weapon. I threw my empty pistol at her as she pulled a book and tossed it at me. Her throw went wide, but mine was spot on; the slide hit her in the face and her head jerked back as she fell. She hit the cold tile floor with her back followed by her head and the thundercrack of her impact sounded painful. Her robe came undone as she tried to catch herself when she fell and her nakedness was all I needed to see to send me into a rage.

I grabbed her by the front of her robe and yanked her up. The silk ripped as I dragged her across the floor. She screamed and I lifted her, holding her out the window as the air rushed by. Far, far below us, the city sounds of running engines passing by gave way to the first sirens following the flashing lights that pulled up at the entrance of the building. "Where is he, Ariadne?"

Her hair whipped around her, falling in lines across her frightened face. "I don't know!"

"I don't see your girlfriend." I looked over the cityscape. "I believe she left you behind to save her own sweet ass." I tightened my hold, shook her slightly, and listened to the fabric tear a little more. "She must really care for you to bail out the window and leave you to fend for yourself."

"She ..." Ariadne looked down in a sidelong glance, considering her options. I could tell she didn't like them, but she still spat defiance when she looked back at me. "You shot her!"

I shrugged lightly, causing Ariadne's weight to shift and drawing another scream from her. The first tears were drawn from her eyes now, rolling down her cheeks and into her hair. I wondered if they would fall from there, all the way down, twenty-eight stories like a drop of rain. "What your boss did to me was worse. Where is he?"

There was another loud rip, and I knew the fabric in the back of her robe was reaching the point of no return. If it broke now, she would fall, and I doubted I'd be able to catch her. There was an enthusiastic chorus of approval from three of the voices in my head at this idea, but I could almost hear Zack screaming at me not to do it.

I ignored him.

"Last chance, Ariadne," I said. "I wouldn't struggle too much. It might hasten your demise. It's kinda like what happened with me after your girlfriend carted you off that night at the Directorate; I struggled and I struggled, but it didn't do me one bit of good."

"I'm ... telling the truth ..." her voice was choked, and something occurred to me, something that would be at once more satisfying and cut right to the truth all in one.

"All right," I said, and I yanked her in then threw her to the floor where she landed, hard. I squatted over her as she tried to escape. "Let's see if that's true." I put my weight on her and pushed her down, felt the cold tile on my hand as I rested against it and lifted the other menacingly in front of her face; her eyes had finally calmed slightly after I brought her back in, but they widened at the sight of my bare fingers.

"No," she said, almost pleading, "No—"

"Funny," I said, thrusting my hand against her cheek, "that's what I said, too. It didn't do me much good, either." I pushed her face against the floor as I waited for my touch to do its work. I felt the first swirl of feeling as it began to move, her memories to mine, the first screams of pain from her as I felt the rush, felt my skin drinking her essence. My head began to swirl with the pleasure of it, and I waited as the screaming became louder, shifting to my head, but instead of being a discordant, ear-shattering howl it was more like music, sweet honey poured into my mind. My powers weren't a torment, not to me, and Ariadne's pain became my pleasure as they started to work, and I let it take over as I drank her, until the screaming finally stopped.

Thirteen

"I want you to go to South America."

The air was clear, the ground covered with snow again, and I could tell by the glare of the sun I was in Ariadne's office. I sat, watching, insubstantial again. The smell of the place was crisp; more Zack's cologne, which caused Ariadne to cringe, than anything else. It was late in the day, and there was a sound of Ariadne tapping the desk with long fingernails as she spoke. I could taste the head of the pen that she was chewing, the bitter flavor of the plastic filtering through as I watched her gnaw on it. I would have considered it odd that I could taste what she was tasting even as I watched her from outside her body, but this was her memory, not mine, and in truth I only wanted to see what she had seen, I didn't really care about the finer details.

"Sorry, what?" Zack asked, blinking across the desk at her.

"I want you to go to South America to get M-Squad," Ariadne said, and I realized that this memory I was seeing was long before Zack's little interlude in the bar, but after his meeting with Old Man Winter where he was told to get close to me. "They're out of contact trying to wrangle a meta named Aleksandr Gavrikov, and we need them to help settle this Wolfe matter. This is of far more importance than Gavrikov, so I need you to get down there and re-establish contact. Bring them home so we can deal with this ... Wolfe situation."

Zack looked slightly rumpled across the desk from me. "Um ... I mean, the Director made it clear to me that my current role was to get closer to the girl—"

"Her name is Sienna," Ariadne said simply. "And you may

carry out whatever order the Director gave you," ice frosted over her tone and I could sense the distaste for the Director's order both in her head and in her tone, "when you get back, if he still wants to go through with that particular ..." She didn't finish her sentence but I heard what she wanted to say in her mind—*obscenity*.

"Um, all right," Zack said, and stood. "I'll ... uh ..."

"There'll be a helicopter waiting in a half hour," she said, coolly watching him. "Be on it."

"Okay," he said with a nod, and I looked at the lines of his face. He was handsome, no doubt, and I caught the hint from his look that he knew something else was going on, something with Ariadne giving him this order. He walked out without saying anything else, and the world changed dramatically in the moments after that. It took me a moment to realize that I was seeing time leap forward—the sun went down, the office became dark, shadows creeping in around the light cast by the fluorescents overhead. Ariadne sat there, her pen scratching out ink letters on a page in front of her.

"You sent Zack Davis away," came the rumble from the door, and Ariadne looked up.. The chill had crept into the room preceding him, and I saw Ariadne fold her arms across her chest, partially out of a sense of defense and partly to warm herself from the rush of cold air.

"I did," she said, pulling her arms tighter around her. "He's on his way to retrieve M-Squad from South America. He should be back in a day or two."

"I see," Old Man Winter answered coldly. "And did you do this because of my orders to him to get closer to the girl?"

"No," Ariadne said, and I knew that she was lying. Winter knew it, too, I was sure, but he said nothing. "He was available. A grunt, but one we've trusted with more responsibility. He seemed the one to do it."

"Is that so?" Erich Winter asked, his towering figure taking up the whole of the door frame. "I have taken the opportunity to use this to our advantage."

Ariadne froze in a way that had nothing to do with the cold in the room. "Oh?"

"Yes," Erich Winter said, "I've had him say a farewell to the girl that involved extracting a promise to remain here, on the grounds, until he can get back. It should give her some hope and allow us to keep her here just a bit longer. Perhaps it will give us some time to solve the mystery of what type of meta she is, which will perhaps give us some insight into why Wolfe is pursuing her as aggressively as he is."

Ariadne brought her pen up, but halted it an inch from the outside of her mouth. "He's working for someone, isn't he?"

"Oh, yes," Winter said, "but the question is 'who?' And also … 'why' is she so important to them?" Winter shook his head. "Wolfe has always been a dangerous foe, and his choices of employers is always carefully considered. He has served a dozen masters in the time I have known him, each dangerous in their own way, all of them a threat to whomever they considered their enemies." Winter's eyes narrowed. "This time feels different, though; whoever has sent him here has done so for reasons that he has left behind him. Wolfe wants to hurt the girl, now, to make her suffer because she has hurt him. He does not countenance any sort of will being turned against him; he considers it a challenge to break resistance that is offered to him. Whoever his employer is, he is not heeding their wishes at this point, I would wager. He will not take the girl unharmed, though whatever remains of her when he is done may eventually be offered to them."

Ariadne's voice was low when she answered. "But we're going to protect her, right?"

"For a time," Winter said. "We will keep her safe, for now, and try to determine what she is."

Ariadne frowned. "Wait. For a time?"

Old Man Winter gave a little shrug. "She is of some import, to someone, somewhere. We need to find out who at some point. If we cannot gather these answers ourselves, the natural conclusion is to find a way to track her … and then make certain Wolfe gets his hands on her."

Ariadne sat back in her chair, her brow furrowed as she stared at Old Man Winter in sickly disbelief. "I thought we were going to protect her. That's why we're here, to protect metas, to keep the entire species out of danger by policing them—"

"We have many purposes," Old Man Winter said darkly, "and protecting one at the expense of more is doing us no service." He began to turn but Ariadne made a noise that caused him to stop and survey her with his cold blue eyes. "What?"

"You knew the girl … Sienna … you knew her mother, didn't you?" The pen was no longer resting in Ariadne's mouth. Now it was clenched in her hand.

"I did." He watched coldly. "What of it?"

Ariadne swallowed visibly, and I could see her taking care with her words. "Her mother was the one who betrayed the Agency and caused it to be destroyed? While you were there?"

Winter's eyes narrowed. "It seems likely that she gave us over to …" There was a flash of frost in his eyes. "To destruction."

"What destroyed the Agency?" Ariadne asked. "You never talk about it." She let out a small laugh, which was no louder than a sigh. "You never talk about anything, but especially not that."

Winter's cold eyes faded as though looking far off. "It was not a simple 'what' that destroyed the Agency. It was a 'who.'"

Ariadne blinked, almost flinching. "You mean one of the old-world meta organizations?"

"No," Old Man Winter said. "A person. One man."

Ariadne's face furrowed, lines stitching the slight wrinkles that barely showed around her face. "One meta, I presume?" Old

Man Winter nodded. "How is that even possible? I thought the Agency had a hundred metas at their disposal for all manner of tasks—"

"We did," Winter said. "We did indeed. And one meta … was all it took to undo it all, to turn a facility twice the size of this one into utter wreckage and kill every metahuman in the entire place save for two."

"You and … Sierra, I think her name was?" Ariadne waited for Old Man Winter to nod. "But how did you escape?"

Old Man Winter's head slumped, subtly. Anyone who didn't know him that saw it would think nothing of it; that it was a slight nod, a nearly insubstantial incline of his jaw. But to those of us who knew him … even after the surprise he'd given me recently, I knew somehow … that this was his feeling of defeat. "Because," Old Man Winter said, "he let me live." The blue eyes came up, glowing again, with a cold fury. "And he told me so. There was no need for him to prove his dominance over me, to assert his superiority." Winter leaned back against the door frame as though hurt, and his fingers went to his torso, massaging the material of his dress shirt as though he could rub at an old wound beneath.

"I don't understand," Ariadne said, looking at him with undisguised curiosity. "If he killed the rest, why would he let you live?"

"Because," Old Man Winter said, now holding his shoulder as though it pained him, "he had already broken me … before." Without allowing for further explanation, he turned, leaving Ariadne in her office, and returned to his own. The slow, quiet sound of the door closing in the next office was almost as loud as an explosion as Ariadne stayed there, alone, pondering the complete incongruity of what he had said.

I watched too, insubtantial, and thought about what he had said, and waited to wake up.

Fourteen

I blinked back to awake, the orange light of sunset barely edging through the curtains. I had slept the whole day away. I hadn't gotten home until nearly six in the morning, after dodging out of the apartment building through a back exit on the first floor. The sheets didn't smell of sweat this time, but the pall of my night's activity still hung in the air, and I checked the nightstand next to me. Two pistols still lay upon it, within easy reach if I needed them. I sighed a deep sigh.

Having seen Ariadne's memory in my dream was enough to get me wondering about the Agency. It had been a mystery to me, what happened to it, especially since my mother hadn't told me all that much. I tried to sift through what I knew, but it was so minimal it wasn't really worth hashing it over. The only concrete thing I knew was that my father had died there. "Any of you know about the Agency and how it was destroyed?" I asked the empty house.

Yes, Little Doll, Wolfe said.

Only rumors, Bjorn added. Gavrikov remained quiet, which made me wonder about him; I supposed he was still upset with me about what I'd said about his sister. I didn't care.

"All right, Wolfe, spill it." I leaned back on my bed and stared at the white ceiling.

The Agency was destroyed by angry metas, Bjorn said. *A cloister in South Dakota, furious over the Agency taking some of their own and arresting them—*

"Wait," I said, blinking. "Where was the Agency located?"

In Minneapolis, Wolfe answered helpfully.

"Wouldn't their destruction have made some sort of news? I mean, if there was a battle or riot or whatever?" I asked.

Very artful cover-up, Bjorn went on. *The U.S. Government wanted no record of their failure of the policing structure they had set up for metas, and so they buried it, pretended the whole thing never happened, and turned the entire location into tract housing.*

"I don't buy how it happened," I said. "Did either of you see the dream I just had?" There was a strange feeling of them shaking their heads in my mind. "Old Man Winter told Ariadne that it was one meta who did it." There was a stark silence in my mind. "And I got the feeling—nothing definite—that the guy who destroyed the Agency was the same one who crippled Winter."

There was a slow quiet inside me that I might have found excellent at any other time. "Uh ... guys?"

No, Little Doll, Wolfe said. *No meta is powerful enough to—*

No, Bjorn said, and Wolfe stopped speaking. *There is one. The leader of Century.*

Not important, Wolfe said, and I got the feeling he was trying to distract me. I tried to decide whether I should let him or not. *Only one thing matters right now and that's the Little Doll's revenge.* I felt a flare of anger, and I hated to disagree with him ... really hated it. I felt a visceral reaction, a tightening of the muscles in my abdomen, a taste of bitter on my tongue, and I wondered if he'd been manipulating me all this time, pushing me in the direction he'd wanted me to go. I knew in a flash that he had, because he felt my thought and tried to backpedal, receding into the recesses of my mind.

"You've been playing games with me, Wolfe," I said in slight shock. "I knew you ... I knew you could take over my body when I slept before, but ... you've been doing things to me while I'm awake ...

Nothing, Little Doll, nothing the Wolfe expected you to notice. Subtle things, almost not there.

"You're touching my emotions," I said with disgust, "you're playing with them, flaring my anger when you want me mad—"

And flooding you with adrenaline when need be, don't forget that, and burning off your fear when you feel it at the wrong time. The rasp was there, in his voice, in my head. *The Wolfe is good to the Little Doll. Takes care of her. Looks out for her and keeps her out of trouble.*

I felt my head loosely fall into my hands. "Oh, God, what have I been doing?" I let myself peek between my fingers and look at the blank wall on the opposite side of the bedroom. "Have you been running me this whole time?" There was a quiet in which I felt panic that was not my own. "This whole thing ... all this revenge, these killings ... this was all your idea."

No, no, Wolfe said and Bjorn joined in the chorus. *Wolfe was only showing the doll the way, never had to do any of it for her, hardly at all. Only showed her, helped her, guided her. Got her out of a few jams.*

"You pushed me into it," I said numbly. "You knew how I was feeling and—"

Despair is a very useless emotion, Little Doll. Makes you feel powerless, keeps you in chains—in a box, in your case. Anger could break the doll out of it, if she used it. Wolfe waited, tried to see if the Little Doll would find it on her own, but she didn't. So Wolfe only ... gave her a little push. Just a little shove in the right direction. Wanted to make her powerful again, not weak and mewling. I caught a hint of disgust, but whether it was from him or me I didn't honestly know.

I buried my face in my hands. "I'm not some broken girl that needs to be saved by the crazies in my head." There was no answer to this, as if they were fearful of my response, but the undercurrent was there, just the same; strong disagreement, like the rolling of the eyes. "I'm not some ... some shattered mess that can't ..." I felt my eyes tear up and I clenched a fist, sending a hard breath out through my teeth as though I could push the unwanted emotion out that way. "I … I won't fall apart. Not now. Not ever."

Little Doll already fell apart, I heard Wolfe's voice tell me. *She fell apart, broken, and dragged herself back to a place she swore she would never go, locked herself in the dark, punished herself for all the wrongs she'd ever done, and swore she'd never come out again. The Little Doll's heart was broken; her fate was set, and she surrendered herself to die, to waste away locked in the dark for all the days of her life.*

"No," I said, shaking my head, trying to cast off the weight of the feelings that were bearing down on me hard now. "I'm not … I'm not broken. Not yet. I can hold it together. I can. I didn't need your help, your push. I'm just … hurt. Just a little damaged. But I'll make them pay, and that will fix …" I heard the hollow sound of my voice, trying to persuade me, "… fix … everything." I didn't even believe it when I finished saying it.

Worse than the hollow words that echoed in my ears was the silence that followed from the voices in my head. It was a silence that told me that every one of them was sure I would have been finished if not for their help—and no more likely to be put back together than anything else that had been irreparably destroyed.

Fifteen

It was after nightfall when I pulled into the parking lot of yet another bar. I was in a town called Hamel, Minnesota, and the bar was a faded white building with cracking paint. It wasn't as showy as the one I'd been in a few days earlier when I met Kurt, but then this place wasn't the same, either. It was a small town, and I could see both sides of it from where I'd parked on the main street. In a way it reminded me of Glencoe, a town that wasn't even there anymore, one that I'd been the last living person to leave. I filed that thought away for later, hoping that random memory was completely unrelated to what I was about to experience here. Snow was coming down all around me now, clinging to my hair as I crossed the quiet main street. It was late—after eleven but before midnight—and it had been snowing for a few hours now.

I stepped into the quiet room, scanning the entire place in one smooth movement. I found my target, in the corner, his back to me and a beer hoisted in the air in front of him. He had a crowd with him, and it was the only table in the place that was occupied. It was a weeknight, and these were the hardcore drinkers, the ones who drank every night of the week. He was right in the middle of them, just one of the guys. I tried to decide what to do about that, and finally figured I'd just walk up and tap him on the shoulder.

Before I could even get halfway across the room, he turned to the bartender. "Hey! Another round for my friends!" His sandy-blond hair came off his scalp in curls, and the faux smile on his face might have fooled almost anyone else but not me. He was sloshed and wearing a kind of fake-happy grin that kept him going through one drink after another. He waved at the barman, who was already in motion, as a chorus of cheers and hoisted glasses around the table in the corner let me know what his companions thought of his generosity.

One of the drunks at his table who was facing me was the first to notice my approach. I wasn't wearing the sunglasses, but I did have on my long black coat, and so far as I knew, I probably looked like some lesser version of the angel of death. The first one to see me nudged the guy next to him in the ribs with an elbow, and one by one the table quieted down until the only one still talking boisterously was the one I was here to see.

"Hey," one of his compatriots interrupted him as I hovered behind the blond-haired man. "Someone's here to see you." The guy stood and glared me down. "You aren't … Kat … .are you?" There was a touch of menace in his voice.

I would have rolled my eyes at him, but instead I fired off the hardest glare I could imagine as Scott Byerly swiveled in his chair to face me, his head dipping enough that I knew he'd already had plenty to drink. "Kat?" he said as he saw me. I caught the millimeter fall in his facial expression from disappointment before he spoke again. "No, guys, this isn't Kat. This is Sienna." He let out a low, unserious laugh. "They are not the same person at all." He paused a beat. "Thank God."

"Thank Him once for me as well," I said, standing over Scott with my arms crossed.

Scott laughed again, but it wasn't mirthful. "You should join us. We were just drinking."

"I noticed that. What with this being a bar and all, I figured it was down to either drinking or darts, and I remembered you're not very good with small objects when you're loaded, and I could smell the alcohol on you from across the bar."

He squinted at me. "Wait, what?"

I let out an impatient sigh. "I was a making small penis joke."

"Oh." He frowned. "That's not very nice."

"You were expecting nice from me? How hammered are you?" He shrugged and I tossed a thumb toward the bar. "Can I talk to you?"

He wobbled in his seat but managed to stand, casting a look back at the men behind him. "I'll be back in a minute. Don't go anywhere without me."

"They won't," I said. "Where else are they going to find an idiot to buy them free drinks all night?"

Scott nodded. "It's true." He shrugged at them. "Back in a few."

I led him over to the bar and he pushed himself onto the stool and made a motion to the bartender for two drinks. The bartender, already filling his last order, nodded, stopped and made his way down to us with shot glasses. "Drink with me, Sienna," Scott said as the bartender put the glasses in front of us and poured an amber liquid into them.

"That doesn't seem like a winning idea to me," I said as I looked at the drink, the strong smell of alcohol hanging over it like a cloud, almost causing my eyes to tear up. "Maybe I'll stick with water."

"Boooo," he said, slurring. "It's bad luck to toast with water."

"Do you feel like there's been an overabundance of luck that's come our way of late?" I looked at him with what might have been a wry smile once upon a time, but now it felt more like a leer. He stared at me, and I saw the smoky hint of something in his eyes. "You know, don't you?"

He looked away, took the shot from in front of him and downed it in one swift motion, his lips pulling together in a grimace after he was done. "Jackson came over to drink with me a day or two ago, told me about what went down." He looked at me out of the corner of his eye as he motioned for a refill. "Sorry about Zack."

"I'm sorry about Kat," I said, not really sincere. "Did you

ever hear how that one turned out?"

He looked at me with a frown. "I heard she and Dr. Perugini are missing and presumed dead in the destruction of the campus."

I eyed him, then nudged the shot glass from in front of me to in front of him. "She's alive and well, and a full-on Omega lackey."

The shot glass was almost to Scott's lips when he dropped it out of his hand. He didn't bother to step back as it hit the floor and splattered whiskey all over his jeans and shoes. "She what?"

"She's back to who she was before Kat," I said. "Back to working for Omega, I guess. She betrayed us."

Scott leaned forward, putting his elbows on the bar. "Jackson didn't … mention that." I saw a waver of uncertainty. "Does she remember me?" I caught the note of hope.

I didn't pull the punch. "No. Not really."

He let that sink in then looked at me sideways. "How did you find me?"

"Ariadne," I said. "She was tracking you for some reason."

"Nice," he said with a look back to the bottles behind the bar. "Probably trying to figure out a way to make me drown my ex-girlfriend so she could send me over the edge." I flinched and he caught it, and gave me a look of apology. "Sorry." The barman sat another shot in front of him and he took it, fast. "But in all seriousness, I doubt I'd need a ton of motivation to do her in at this point, especially if she's working with Omega now."

We stood there in silence for a moment. The bartender refilled Scott's glass, and at his urging put another one in front of me. I thought about waving him off; I didn't like the taste of alcohol, didn't like the effects, didn't care for any of it. Ultimately, though, I let it lie there, looked at the glass, smelled the pungent aroma, and listened to the jukebox keep going in the background of the near-empty room. "I've been in and around a lot of bars lately. What do you make of that?"

"Must be something in our chosen profession," Scott said. "Something that makes a body want to drink heavily."

I thought about it for a moment. "You know, you might have something there."

He cast an accusing eye toward the shot occupying the bar in front of me. "Yet still you remain as sober as a priest."

I took a sniff of the alcohol wafting off the shot in front of me. "Probably the memory of what happened to me last time I wasn't." I gave a slight shrug. "They say judgment is the first thing to go."

He laughed, a sound so bereft of any amusement I wondered if it might be better called a bark. "What are you up to, Sienna?"

"Me?" I stared at the drink in front of me and thought about lying. "I'm going to kill Old Man Winter."

There was a pause. "Good for you."

"You really mean that?"

"I don't know," Scott said, and I saw a line of water drip down the shot glass in his hand. "I know I'd like to have a convenient target for my emotional toxic waste." He sighed. "I can't even hate her. She saved my life, because of that dumb bastard Clary—" He turned to me. "I could hate him."

I watched him carefully. "You could. But he's dead."

Scott didn't even bat an eyelash, just looked at me with undisguised curiosity. "Did you?"

I looked back at the drink and took it, slopping it down in one. I slapped the glass back down on the bar and cringed as the alcohol burned all the way down. "I did."

His expression settled, going from a kind of muted rage to relaxed. "I'd say, 'Good for you' but I kind of doubt it actually is any good for you."

"It doesn't feel very good," I conceded. "I got Parks and Clary. I had Eve, filled her with bullet holes, but she got away. That leaves her, Bastian and ..." I let my jaw harden, "the man himself."

He looked at me and I could see the wheels turning for him. "Do you think he was playing us all along?"

I cocked my head at him. "What do you mean?"

"I mean Winter strung us along, right?" Scott's hand came off his glass and he gestured wildly. "He made you think he was on your side all along, and then bam—kills your boyfriend. Do you think he ever actually gave a damn about us or was he just playing some sort of game that only he knew about?"

"I don't know," I said. "I think he did what he did for reasons that he didn't share. He wanted me to kill, to 'do what was necessary,'"I said in a faux Old Man Winter accent. "I don't know that he ever cared, though. I think he was always focused on his own means, this war with Omega and Century and whoever else. The storm, my mom called it. We were just the tools for him to use to get whatever he needed out of it."

"So did we do any good?" Scott asked, as the barman refilled our glasses. "Was there any point to all the training, the missions? I mean, the Directorate's toast, so I guess Omega wins, right?"

"Reed's still out there, somewhere in Rome," I said, thinking of my brother. "I don't know how to get ahold of him, but he's out there. Alpha's probably still fighting them, in Europe. All that other stuff is still going on, some other group—Century they're called—they wiped out all those metas in China and India. So I don't know. Maybe Omega did win. At least, between that and what happened afterward, I don't know where I fit anymore." I felt a snarl curl my lips. "I guess I'm on my own side, now."

"That's a tough place to be in a fight like this," Scott said. "We were always the little kids playing in the old gods' play yard, though, right?"

I stared straight ahead at the bottles behind the bar. "I guess. I don't know."

"Well," Scott said with an air of making a great

pronouncement, and I saw him looking me over, "it sounds like you made a good start with Parks and Clary. But … if you missed Eve, I'm betting she's working with Bastian and Winter. They know you're coming now, right?"

"Yep."

"So, are you gonna finish it?" Scott was watching carefully for my reaction.

"I dunno," I said. "There are other factors in play."

"Like what?" he asked.

"Like that since I can't get my hands on my medication anymore, I'm not the only one steering my course." I said it glumly, and felt it all the way through me.

Scott didn't answer for a minute. "You mean … if you didn't have other voices in your head, you wouldn't want to get them back for what they did to Zack?"

"Zack was a paid plant," I said quietly. "Winter told him from the beginning to get close to me." I leaned in closer to the bar, and considered the fresh drink the barman had placed in front of me. It didn't smell so bad, now.

"Holy shit," Scott said in awe and took down this shot faster than any of the others. He remained quiet and pensive for a moment, then turned back to me. "I don't buy it."

"Don't buy what?" I asked. "I saw Zack's memory. I saw the meeting where it happened."

"Could be Wolfe," Scott said, "he could be feeding you something to make you—"

"Make me what?" I said with an odd smile. "Make me not want to kill? Wolfe wants me to kill. It's his purpose in afterlife."

Scott rested fingers on his chin, which I noticed had the hints of sandy stubble upon them. "I just don't believe it, I'm sorry. I knew Zack. I saw him look at you. He—"

"Stop," I said quietly, and smiled a fake smile. "I appreciate it, but stop. I'm gonna do what I'm gonna do. If I go after Winter

… and I'm leaning toward it … it'll be for me, not for Zack." I felt my jaw harden again. "It'll be for what he did to me, not what he did to … anyone else."

"Gotta love a girl who can settle her own account," Scott said. He looked back to the bartender, who was a few feet away now. "In this case, though, her drink's on me." He looked at the still-full shot resting in front of me. "Both of them and more, if she wants them."

"I think I'm done," I said, and pushed back from the bar, getting up off the stool. "What about you? You just gonna hang out here for the rest of your life?"

He smiled, a faint one. "What life? I wanted to be a member of M-Squad since the day I learned what I was, which was … a long time ago. Probably since my parents first sent me to the Directorate at thirteen. It's all I ever wanted." He took a drink, just a sip this time. "Now I don't want to be anything like them. Or at least what's left of them." He put the shot glass down. "I hope you kill them for what they did to you. I hope you kill 'em all."

"What are you gonna be doing?" I asked. "Hanging out here?"

He gave a loose shrug, but I saw the sadness in his eyes. "At night, yep. During the day, I sleep. Keep repeating the cycle until something else comes up."

"And the war?" I pointed toward the door. "What about what's going on out there?"

He let only a faint amusement show. "I don't know. What are you gonna do about it?"

I deflated slightly. "I don't know. It all feels … so much bigger than me or you, doesn't it?"

He nodded and picked up his glass again. "Yep. Just a couple of little pieces in a very, very big game. One that's way too big for me to navigate my way into alone."

I shrugged. "You know someone in Omega, now. You could

always ask to go with them."

He got a sour look. "I haven't forgotten Wolfe and what he did to my aunt and uncle. Nor Henderschott, or Fries, those vampires ..." He frowned. "Was Gavrikov with Omega?"

"Before he came looking for Kat, yeah, I think so. He was with them from way back."

"I hate 'em," he pronounced. "I hate everything about them— what they've done, the people they've used. I couldn't trust them. I *wouldn't* trust them. If Reed came back and asked me to fight for Alpha, I'd go with him. You know, after I've gotten all this out of my system." He tipped his glass back. "I trust him, and I trust you." His eyes grew glazed. "And that's about it, I'm sad to say."

I didn't know what to say to that, so I just stared at him. "I'm sorry it came to this."

"So am I," Scott said. "I really am sorry about Zack. If I was betting man—and, hey I kinda am—I would bet you any amount of money that you're wrong about him."

"It's kind of you to say." I walked backward, careful not to trip over a table on my way out the door. "But I know what I've seen." I felt my voice harden. "And I know what I have to do."

"You don't have to do anything, Sienna," Scott called to me as I reached the door. "Whatever you're doing, it's you who's choosing it. Remember that."

"I will," I said, and gave him a last look as I clutched the handle to the door of the bar. The whiskey smell hung thick in the air, and the crowd in the corner was watching me leave, looking at Scott furtively, expectantly, wondering if he was going to return to them now. I smiled. "I kinda doubt, based on your current condition, that you'll remember this conversation tomorrow, though."

He smiled back, and it was the warmest look I could remember seeing anyone give me since the morning I actually woke up with my boyfriend still alive at my side. It hadn't even been a week, but it felt like forever ago already. "I find it hard to forget you, Sienna Nealon." He raised his glass. "You've saved my life a few too many times for me to do you that particular disservice." His smile faded. "But you wouldn't be the first if you didn't remember me."

"I can't forget you, Scott," I said as I opened the door and felt the cold air hit me hard as I walked out, feeling the first crunch of my boot in the snow. "After all, you're the only actual friend I think I have left."

Sixteen

I hit my stride walking to my car and I slammed the door once I got inside. It was sad to consider but probably true; other than Reed, Scott was probably the last person I actually liked on the face of the planet. Everyone else was persona non grata to me or on my list of people I was actively trying to kill. I cursed loudly to the empty car, furious at myself again for letting Eve get away. I'd had a chance, and I taunted her just a little too long. I should have finished her and trusted that Kurt would find Bastian and Winter for me later. It wasn't the first mistake I'd made; I hoped it wouldn't lead to my last, but frankly, I didn't care all that much if it was, so long as I knocked the last three things off my bucket list first.

I pondered going somewhere but felt the soft buzz of the whiskey I'd had and knew it was a bad idea. I leaned my head back against the seat and took a sniff. Zack's faint smell was beginning to fade, the car's cloth seats gradually giving up their former master's scent as time went by and I used it more and more. I tried to find reassurance in that, but there was none; whatever else Zack had done to me, he'd made me love him. "Mission accomplished, Winter," I said out loud. "You dick."

I didn't even realize I had slipped off to sleep until I saw myself somewhere else, again as formless as every other memory I'd lived through. Kurt was there, sitting beside Zack in a car. He looked over at his younger partner, almost guilty. "You know what he had me do, right?" I heard the little bit of acid in his tone, like he despised someone.

"I just got back," Zack said. "Thrilling vacation in South

America, you know, where I almost got fried by a man who catches his own skin on fire. I have no idea what's going on."

Kurt reached for his own head, massaging the scalp. "Yeah, well, not three hours ago I got the holy hell clubbed out of me by a guy wearing an oversized soup can. Count your blessings."

Zack gave him a subtle nod. "You were talking about Winter?"

"Yeah," Kurt said. "And that girl." He swore. "That friggin' girl, I swear—"

Zack laughed. "Don't let her get to you, man. She's seventeen. She's probably writing in her diary right now, 'I hate that Kurt guy, he's a big meanie.'"

Hannegan stared at him grudgingly. "You got a point. Count yourself lucky you didn't try and sleep with her before you took off for South America."

"Yeah," Zack said, indifferent. "No kidding. I felt it, you know. I took her hand before I left, when I was saying goodbye. I got all lightheaded when I tried to stand up but I had no idea it was from that. I figured the pain in my hand was just delayed from when I tangled with Wolfe."

"And by tangled, you mean when you got your ass kicked."

"Yeah," Zack said. "So anyway, what was the deal?"

"When she was in containment," Kurt said, and looked around, as though there were someone in the car with them, "Winter had me go down there to taunt her, goad her, then offer to spring her. He wanted me to play on her guilt from being able to see everything that was happening on the news. He told me what to say, how to say it." Hannegan shook his head. "They've been feeding her a steady diet of misery while she was down there, making her feel guilty."

"Who?" Zack looked at him with unconcern. "Ariadne?"

"Maybe her, too," Kurt said, waving him off, "but definitely Winter. He wanted her to know what was going on, how many people were dying. And then he goes and tells me to help her get out. I dunno whether he wanted to see if she'd try or if he really wanted her outta here, but he told me to help her escape, and take her wherever she wanted to go if it was here in the cities. So I did. Dropped her off at her house. Turns out he's trailing us the whole time with a squad." Hannegan shook his head in amused disbelief. "We see Wolfe go into her house from a couple blocks away and he just keeps us at a distance. He's got the place bugged from top to bottom, and he's sitting there with one of the tech guys as everything's going on, that stoic face of ice." Hannegan's expression changed, and he smacked his lips together. "He sent her there to die, man. I wouldn't get real attached to that girl, cuz Winter already tried to throw her to the undertaker once." There was almost an expression of guilt on Hannegan's fat face, furtive, almost ashamed. "I mean, she's a little bitch, but—"

"Yeah, that sucks," Zack said with all the interest he might give a pronouncement about the weather.

"Yeah," Hannegan said. "You're not concerned?"

"She's just a job, pal," Zack said, and looked back to the steering wheel. "I do what I'm told. Like playing undercover, y'know. Acting."

"Yeah," Hannegan said, "but didn't he tell you he wanted you to get close to her to get her to stay?"

Zack nodded. "Yeah. And?"

"But then he had me help her throw herself into the path of Wolfe?" Hannegan gave Zack a knowing look. "What do you think the old man's playing at? One minute he saves her, the next he tosses her to the wolves—err ... Wolfe?"

"Who knows?" Zack asked with a light shrug. "It's a job. A weird job, but a job. Pays better than being a city cop, or even an FBI starter like my college roommate."

"Yeah, but if he's that quick to toss one of his own under a bus, do you think he'll ever pull that with either of us?" Kurt eyed

Zack, watching for a response.

"I dunno," Zack said. "Probably tends to make me look over my shoulder a little more carefully, though."

"Smart move," Kurt said, shifting his bulk in the car seat to look straight ahead again. "Seriously, though. I wouldn't get attached to the girl."

"It's just a job, man." Zack put his hands on the wheel. "In addition to being the death of me if I touch her for very long, she's not really my type." He frowned. "And immature. Maybe a little crazy, locked up all those years. Who knows?"

"Yeah, well," Kurt said, "I'm just trying to watch your back, y'know. Somebody should around here."

"I gotcha, buddy," Zack said with a wide, exaggerated smile. "And I'll watch your back, too. We're humans in a meta world; we need all the help we can get, right?"

"I suppose so," Kurt said, and turned his eyes back out the windshield. "I will tell you, though, I'm glad the girl won in that bout with Wolfe. If she kills that bastard in the metal suit, I might almost like her."

"I doubt it," Zack said. "You don't really like anyone."

"I liked you well enough up til now, you jackass."

They both laughed, and the dreamlike quality of the world around me faded into an insistent buzzing sound. I came back to consciousness, in the car, the drowse of sleep clinging to my eyes as I forced them open. A streetlight overhead shed light on me, giving me a view of the parking lot of the bar. I was still here, and when I glanced back, I saw that the place was closed, all the lights off now. Snow had started to fall while I was unconscious, and there was a light dusting already on the ground. I wondered how long I had been asleep when my cell phone buzzed again in my coat. I picked it out of my pocket and thumbed it on, then hit the message indicator. The text was from Kurt, and was as simple as could be.

Meet me at Carlson HQ off 394 and 694 ASAP. Winter is leaving the country TONIGHT. One last chance to get a shot at him and then he's gone; destination unknown.

Seventeen

The car bucked slightly as I pulled it into the parking lot at the Carlson towers. The only other one here was Kurt, leaning up against the side of his car as snowflakes fell around him, illuminated by the lamps in the lot.

I pulled up next to him, keeping myself from actively running him over. I felt a surge of numbness coupled with faint irritation at the sight of him. The fact that it didn't exactly translate into an instant desire to harm him gave me little hope for what was left of my soul, especially since I'd so recently done so much killing.

I threw the door open and took a long sniff of the night air. As I got out, the flakes came down on my shoulder and I felt the tingle on my head as they caught in my hair and started to melt. "Well?" I asked expectantly.

His face was shadowed, his acne scars even more prominent in the darkness. "Well, you've done it now. Eve got away and warned him, so now Winter's fleeing the country. He's out of here in less than an hour."

"Didn't know I could scare him that bad. No idea where he's going?" I asked. I felt a sense of caution; after my most recent dream, I wasn't quite sure where I stood with Kurt.

"Nope." He shook his head. "But he's lost the rest of his security detail except for Eve and Bastian. The other guys bailed on him; Jackson talked them out of showing up." He let a half-smile. "Told 'em it'd be hazardous to their health if they got between you and Winter."

"Remind me to write him a thank-you note after I finish murdering the last of my enemies," I said acidly, and Hannegan's smile disappeared. "Where are they?"

"The airport in Eden Prairie," he said, and any mirth he'd shown was gone. "It's just down the street—"

"From the mall," I said. "I know."

"He chartered a plane," Kurt said soberly. "Like I said, dunno where he's going, but he's getting gone. Eve and Bastian are going with him."

I let out a sordid smile. "I guess Eve really does care more about saving her ass than her girlfriend's."

Kurt didn't really know how to take that. "You killed her, didn't you? Ariadne?"

I rode right past that one. "They got any weapons?"

Kurt looked uneasy, but answered anyway. "Whatever they'd normally have. Probably pistols. Hard to imagine them toting much bigger around the airfield, but I suppose it's possible. They're there now; you might wanna hurry."

"Okay," I said. I turned back to my car, not wanting to look at him as I said the next thing that was on my mind. "You knew all along he was gonna screw me over again, didn't you?"

Hannegan flinched; I could hear it in the pause before his reply. "You found about that first time, huh? With Wolfe? I didn't know he'd do it again. Not for sure, anyway. But then again, with Winter … no one knows what's going on in his head."

I nodded slowly as I turned back to face him. I took a step closer, inches from him. "Let me tell you what's going on in my head right now. I'm gonna take this information you've given me, and I'm gonna make a run at Eve, Bastian and Winter. If I can, I'm going to kill every last one of them. If I fail and they kill me, that's fine. That's the name of the game. If I succeed but they kill me, that's also fine. But if I fail … and I fail because you've screwed me in some way …" I leaned closer and let my bare palm caress Hannegan's pockmarked cheek, "I'll be adding another name to my list." I let him go and walked back to my car.

"It's legit info," Hannegan said, and I stole a look back as I got in the car. He was massaging his face, as though I'd actually hurt him with my touch. "I wouldn't do that to you."

I stared back at him and let my glare hang between us. "Again, you mean." I watched his face dissolve from anger, watched it fall. "You mean you wouldn't do it again." I slammed the door and started the car, and I didn't spare him another look or another thought as I pushed it into gear and down the snow-slicked roads toward Eden Prairie.

Eighteen

The airfield was on a bluff, looking out over a beautiful valley that stretched over the horizon. On a clear day you could see Valley Fair from the top of it. It was a great view, one that Zack and I had enjoyed more than a few times, driving down the road next to the airport and making our way down the slow cliff-road at the far side of it.

I couldn't see any of it in the dark. I made my way to the high fence as the snow continued to fall. It had slowed my drive, taken it down to a slog, twenty miles per hour the entire way, even on the freeway. The plows had yet to start dealing with the mess that Mother Nature had started to dump on the state of Minnesota, but I wasn't sure I cared. I could see a plow running on the airfield, clearing one of the lanes, its big orange front end plow pushing the snow in front of it as it endeavored to make a space for a plane to take off.

I had parked down the road at a gas station and run the rest of the way; with the snow and the cold, I figured I had made it almost as quickly as if I'd driven up to the front gates. I presumed the field was normally closed at this time of night, but they were either making an exception for Old Man Winter or he was ensuring he was the first one to leave in the morning. I didn't really care which, I only cared that he wasn't going to be leaving alive.

I cleared the perimeter fence with a mighty jump and landed in the snow, sparing myself an embarrassing fall by maintaining my balance and footing. It didn't really matter if I faced off with Old Man Winter while covered in snow, I supposed, but my seething fury made me think I'd look more dangerous if I wasn't covered in fresh powder.

There were a cluster of hangars ahead, corrugated metal buildings that screened me from sight of the main runways. I hurried over to them, keeping myself bent low. I had no idea where Eve or Bastian were, or Old Man Winter himself, come to think of it.

My feet crunched in the snow as I ran. A few lights hanging off the sides of the buildings were the sole source of illumination under the dark, snow-filled skies. I listened as I went and paused at the back of the building. I heard something around the corner, footsteps, and I halted, my hands going under my coat as quickly as I could get them there. They emerged with an M4 rifle that I'd pilfered from Parks' stash. I'd carried one from time to time in training and was familiar with it. It had a much better range than any of the submachine guns but wasn't as good at distance as the sniper rifle I'd picked up. That was okay, though. I wasn't planning to be at long range.

I wanted to be up close and personal.

The footsteps edged closer and I held my breath. I needed to be quiet; whoever it was absolutely could not scream, and I needed them to get off a shot like I needed to throw up a fireworks display that announced, "Sienna is here!" I wished briefly for a knife but instead came up with a simple solution, one that would surely have been approved of by Parks had he been here.

I stayed still against the side of the building as the footsteps came closer, light, crunching in the snow. I saw the barrel of a shotgun first, followed by a person, a flash of blond hair as a face ratcheted toward me in shock, a surprised expression plastered across it. By the time it was fully formed, I had already arced the butt of my rifle out and hit Eve Kappler in the temple.

I heard the crack of bones as her skull fractured and her knees failed. I carried through and caught her as she fell. I plunged to my knees in the snow on top of her, ripping her shotgun out of her hand with my free one and sending it skittering against the side of the building I had been leaning against. I cast a furtive glance over my shoulder along the path she had just walked, but no one was behind me. I grabbed her around the throat and dragged her behind the building, holding her tighter than was probably necessary.

Once I had settled her, I kept my fingers coiled around her throat. She was in a daze, barely conscious, but I was choking her. I kept my hand taut around her neck, and watched as her eyes rolled in her head, then burst open as she came back to consciousness. I had my right knee anchoring her left arm into place even as she tried to get it free. My left hand had hers in a vice grip, and my whole weight was distributed across her. She was pinned in the snow, her blond hair pushed down in the mush as I throttled the life out of her while I waited for my power to take effect.

"Sorry, Eve," I whispered. She had no breath with which to speak, and I felt the first strains of my power starting to work. "It wouldn't have been a fair fight if you'd chosen to orchestrate it, so I don't feel the need to play fair now, either." I mashed harder against her larynx and heard it pop, and she made a choked noise. Her eyes were squinted as she struggled for breath. I knew now that she was feeling the pain from both my touch and her impending suffocation. "That's something I learned from you, really, not to play fair. I wish I'd killed you with that stone I threw that time I tore you out of the sky." I looked at her, not harshly, oddly enough. "I could have, that day. Just a little harder throw, I think, would have done it." I felt the swell of the power on my skin, and it made me feel flushed, hot, even as the snow fell around us, gathering on her dark lashes. "Not that it would have changed things, if you hadn't been there the day Old Man Winter … did what he did," I couldn't even bring myself to say it. "But you'd be one less problem I have to deal with now.

The last surge of her came through, now, and I felt the tingle of the moment when her soul ripped free of her body. It would have bothered me, before, only a week or so ago, to feel it, to feel her torn from herself, to listen to her screaming in my head as she left hers, like the sands leaving her part of the hourglass and coming to mine. I reveled in it now, though; it was twice the rush Charlie had told me it was. My head was swimming with enjoyment; it was far better than the whiskey, and I felt a pleasant hum. "Mmmm," I said to the air around me. "You don't taste too bad, Eve. Kinda light. Fluffy." I looked down in the dead eyes of the thing that used to be her and relinquished my grip on her neck. The eyes stared back at me lifelessly as I stood up and brushed off the snow. I didn't bother to close them; I just let them stare off into the dark sky.

I eased along the side of the building, and I heard Wolfe's voice in my head, along with the murmur of silent approval through the thick feeling of euphoria that draining Eve had given me. *So good, Little Doll. Three down.*

The sense of sweet lightness from what I had done held me so tight in its grip that I didn't even care that he called me Little Doll again. Why did it matter? This was what I was supposed to be doing. My powers were there for me to use, after all, and these people I was killing all deserved it, every last one of them. I gripped my M4 tighter as I strode along the side of the building toward the open space ahead, and it was almost as though I could hear a little song playing in my head, soothing me, my skin flushed with the afterglow of what I'd done. "Two to go."

Nineteen

I came around the corner of the building to an open space. The area was well lit, and I could see the plane Winter would be taking as I stayed in the shadow of the building, watching everything that was happening in front of me. It was a smaller model, a Gulfstream, and as the snow fell I watched the massive orange plow with the flashing lights drive down the runway again, spreading salt out the back of it. It looked like a dump truck with a plow fastened to the front, enormous, as though it carried a ton of dirt along with it. I stayed in the shadow, took a deep breath of chill air and smelled it, the scent of cold air itself. The taste of snowflakes was on my tongue, along with a different flavor, something like the last breath of Eve's soul.

The low hum of the plow reached my ears along with conversation. I looked to the open door of the Gulfstream, which had a ramp built into it, and saw a man, one I didn't know, getting inside. "We'll be ready to take off momentarily, sir," he said, very deferentially, to Old Man Winter, who waited at the bottom in nothing but a thin dress shirt—blue, of course. He wore no jacket, only his trousers and shirt, and had his arms folded across his chest.

Winter turned to Bastian, who stood at his side; Bastian was tall and broad, wider across the chest than almost any man I'd ever seen, and it was pure muscle. I had no idea how much of an edge that would give him in a battle with me; nor did I intend to find out. "Get Eve back over here," Winter said, and Bastian nodded. He started to turn toward me, but I was already moving, out of the shadow of the building.

I fired eight shots with rapidity, the crack of the rounds cutting through the quiet night and the bare hum of the plane's engines starting up in the background. Every one of my bullets caught Bastian across that massive chest of his, perfectly aimed. At the last he ended up on the ground, and I fired three rounds at Winter, who staggered from the shots but did not fall.

"I'm afraid Eve will not be able to join you," I said, crossing the distance between us with slow, taunting steps. I fired twice more into Winter's chest, and he slumped to one knee, looking up at me with those cold blue eyes. "On account of the fact that she's dead, in case you missed the inference."

"It was not lost on me," Winter said in a low, gasping voice, looking up at me from the distance between us. There was no blood on his shirt, not where I'd shot him. There was, however, a crust of ice hanging out of the holes where the bullets had ripped the fabric, and it seemed to be steadily growing.

"Sir," I heard in a rasping voice, and looked over to see Bastian still moving, "go."

I tipped the barrel of my gun toward Bastian but stopped short of firing at him; he had been on all fours in the snow, but something was changing as I watched. His chest was jerking, swelling underneath his coat. I fired at him twice and saw the rounds ricochet. I turned them instead toward Winter, who was still slumped, and ripped off the rest of the magazine at him, but his body was encased in a thick coating of ice now, frozen to the bones. All my shots did was chip away at it.

Winter limped away, toward the ramp to the Gulfstream, and I watched Bastian start to return to his feet now, but twice as big as he had been before, his body distorting horribly. His shirt ripped open to reveal wings, and his head and neck grew longer and larger. His legs seemed to fatten out, and a tail extended. He continued to swell, his skin disappearing as it turned to scales, and he grew larger and larger. He reached the size of a four-story building, his skin scaled like a snake, but with feathers around his head, his body elongated like a serpent's, but with wings. He looked like a cross between a bird, a snake and a Chinese dragon, some mythical combination that made me drop the M4 without even bothering to reload.

He stared down at me from far above, bigger than the plane that was supposed to carry him away from me—me, the danger that they had feared, something so miniscule in comparison to what Bastian had become that I wondered why they had worried at all. With a roar of exhaled breath, he knocked me off my feet. I looked up at him, towering above me, and tried to find any reason to hope that I could possibly win against something so grotesque, so large. I wondered why I had ever thought I had a chance; a scared little girl in a world that was so much bigger than I had ever imagined.

Twenty

I quivered below the creature that Bastian had become, not quite shuddering, but my fingers buried in the snow as he towered over me, head atop the tall, snake-like body, wings extended wider than the wings of the Gulfstream. They were feathered, and with a single flap he rose above me, a creature out of a movie that was larger than any life I could imagine.

Get up, Little Doll, I heard Wolfe shout in my ears over the flapping of Bastian's wings.

"I can't!" I cried out, sitting there on my ass, looking up at the thing above me. "I can't beat that!"

Go, Little Doll.

Move, Bjorn said.

You can destroy it, Gavrikov told me.

Go, Zack whispered.

I got haltingly to my feet, my legs unsteady, and Bastian hovered above me, each beat of his wings threatening to throw me back to the ground. "How do I beat something like that?"

Look for weaknesses, Bjorn suggested.

"It's a friggin' flying dragon!" I shouted. "Where the hell am I gonna find a weakness?"

"Don't kill her!" I heard Old Man Winter shout from behind Bastian. He was atop the ramp of the jet, and I wondered if Old Man Winter was a weakness for Bastian. It really didn't matter if he was, because the likelihood I'd be able to reach him with Bastian between us was somewhere between nil and zilch.

"Not being able to kill me is a weakness, I suppose," I whispered.

Bastian swept his tail in a wide arc toward me, as though it were a sock filled with a paperweight that dangled off the end of his body, and I tried to jump it but didn't quite succeed. The tail hit me squarely in the legs and caused me to flip. I landed on my front, my hands catching me. My wrists felt the impact, as did my face, which snapped down and hit the snowy ground. I didn't feel the snow when I hit, though; to me it seemed like I'd been slammed into the asphalt beneath it. My nose started to bleed, and I came to rest with my face in the powder. I wanted to lie there, but as I looked up I saw Old Man Winter still standing atop the ramp, watching me.

"Oh, no you don't, you son of a bitch," I whispered as I spit blood out of my mouth. Bastian remained just above the ground, the gentle flap of his wings keeping him aloft about five feet overhead but little more than that. His tail was at rest now, extended back behind him. Proportionally, he wasn't nearly as long as a snake of his size would be, but he was long enough to look a little like one. I reached under my coat and pulled out a pistol, a bigger-bodied one. I had no idea what I was going to shoot with it, but I suspected the eyes were the only weak point. Assuming I could hit them; they small targets, far away, and in constant motion.

The tail swooped toward me again, but this time I was ready, and I nailed the timing. I jumped and cleared it, catching myself as I landed on my feet in the snow. He threw the tail at me again, like a whip this time, and I dodged right. I fired three shots at his face, but he made no reaction but to hiss and dart toward me with his head.

I lunged to the side, throwing myself into a shoulder roll that spared me from his wrath as he tore into the metal side of the building behind me. He ripped through it easily with the force of his blow, and his head remained there for a moment, the rest of his body still floating a few feet off the ground.

The Gulfstream had started to move now, rolling toward the runway, cutting a path through the snow that lay on this unplowed section of tarmac. I dodged under the flailing Bastian as he ripped his head out the side of the building with a screech of metal being shredded. I pumped my legs as I ran for the Gulfstream Jet. The ramp was already starting to lift, the hydraulics pulling it shut. I cursed and hurried on, trying to catch up with it.

"GET BACK HERE!" The shout was world-ending, as if a lion had roared it but crossed with the subtle hiss of a snake. I looked back in time to see Bastian dive at me jaws first and I leapt aside, just not quite fast enough. He snagged my arm in his mouth as he went, and I felt it. He didn't bury but one or two teeth in my right forearm, but it was enough to make me scream. I felt something flood through me and the pain subsided; I hoped it was adrenaline but I had no idea. Bastian was speeding up now and my arm was trapped in his jaws, dragging the rest of me along for the ride. I had the presence of mind with the pain blotted out to try something, though, and I grabbed hold of one of the long feathers that stuck out of the sides of his head where the gills would be on a fish, and I ripped hard on it. I wasn't trying to pluck it, however, I was trying to use it to pull myself up.

It worked, and I propelled my body up onto the top of his head. I tried to grab hold there, but there was no obvious place to grasp, so I contented myself with pushing my fingers into a neat cleft in his skin where I presumed scales met. I tightened my grip and tried to wrench loose of the biting hold he had my other arm in, but I couldn't really feel it all that well presently. This was not a huge, surprise, though, considering he had a six-inch long tooth squarely through the middle of my arm.

I held on as he took me a little higher. He lifted us about twenty feet into the air, above the Gulfstream, which was taxiing down a snow-covered runway away from where it had been parked. I could see, far in the distance, where the runway they were on turned onto the one that the snowplow had been diligently working to clear. Dimly, I knew that if I didn't somehow reach Winter's plane by the time they made the turn, I would have failed because they'd take off as soon as they hit the clear tarmac, and I'd lose him, possibly forever.

I gripped Bastian tighter as he started to take a turn to my left. He really did remind me of a Chinese dragon. His body fluttered lazily through the air in a way that defied the laws of physics, like no bird I had ever seen was capable of. He curled upright, straightening as though he were turning to spiral up, but I felt his wings falter with the next flap. The Gulfstream was ahead of us, and he had seemed to be going for it, but the next flap was weaker still, and I heard Bastian exhale in pain.

I realized, just barely, that I felt a surge of something through my hand where I gripped his skull. It was my power at work, again, and I felt the tingle through me, the sweet surge of something like endorphins as I felt my fingers start to draw him out. "Looks like you're not as thick-skinned as Clary, Roberto," I breathed as Bastian began to sink back toward the ground, each subsequent flap of his wings doing less and less to hold him aloft. The sound of the wind was mingled with the howling noise of his consciousness being absorbed into mine. He didn't scream, at least not at first, but when he did, it was a fearsome bellow that shook the world around me.

Bastian sank, closer and closer to the ground, his body beginning to shrink as we came down. My feet hit the snow-covered tarmac with a soft squish, and the snowflakes that were falling made me blink every few seconds and keep my head down. His body was returning to human, a bizarre, slow transformation that was punctuated with pained grunts from him that grew in intensity as the seconds wore on. He tried to batter me away but I held tight as his scales turned back to skin, and the place where I had gripped him turned back into his forehead. He had my arm in his mouth but let it go as it became too much for him and with a last surge I felt him go limp and I dropped his body to the ground as the pleasant swirl in my head took over.

I left his naked corpse behind as I started to run, the natural high of my powers blotting out the pain in my right arm where he'd impaled it. I didn't even look at it as I took off through the snow. The Gulfstream was ahead, I could see it, and all I needed to do was break a window and I'd officially put a serious damper on their travel plans. I wasn't surprised the charter pilot had kept going after what was happening on the runway, but I doubted he'd be dumb enough to attempt to fly away with a depressurized cabin.

The plane was taxiing slowly across the snowy runway, breaking to the crossover with the freshly plowed one. The snow wasn't coming down too thick now, just a little here and there, a break in the storm. The pilot would have to get above the clouds or he'd be risking flying through this soup. Not a good risk, in my opinion, but then, I wasn't a pilot. Actually, I hadn't even been on a plane. I hoped my assumptions were correct.

I ran toward the left wing of the plane, staying well clear of the jet engines mounted to the tail. I caught up with it about a hundred yards from the turnaround and leapt onto the wing. I caught my balance and steadied myself as I saw the cabin door begin to open. I pulled a pistol and pointed it toward the closest window, then started to compensate my aim for the movement of the plane.

There was a heavy thump and Old Man Winter was there, only feet away from me. I emptied the whole magazine at his face without hesitation. Most of them hit, but he had effectively iced his entire skin, like armor, and all it succeeded in doing was chipping at it, putting cracks in the sheet that extended all around his nose and cheeks. "So, that's how it's gonna be," I muttered as I tossed the gun aside. He watched it sail off the edge of the wing; I wasn't concerned, I had two more if I needed them.

I came at him with a rush of anger, his blue eyes barely visible under the ice he'd formed over his body like a protective carapace. I hit him with the palm of my hand and splintering cracks appeared like spiderwebs all across the surface of it. He moved fast but not fast enough, and I dodged his counterpunch by sliding to the side. I punched him again, this time in the side of the head with a blow that had lifetime's worth of fury behind it, and the ice around his ear cracked, breaking off in a fist-sized chunk. I hit him again, and again, watching the breakage spread. I watched little cubes fall off as I hammered at him. "I bet you're handy at a party," I told him as I hit him again and broke loose a three-inch segment of ice. "Y'know, because running out of ice is a persistent concern."

He tried to backhand me but missed as I dodged out of his reach. The sheet of ice coating his face had begun to slide off, damaged now beyond his ability to repair. He pulled it free, revealing a nose that seeped almost black-red blood down his upper lip. "Yes, I did understand your witticism."

"It's hard to tell, with you," I said, and launched into a kick that caught him in the belly. I felt the blow land and I would have sworn it was the hardest kick I'd ever thrown. I heard the break of ice and he doubled over, but recovered quickly and swiped for me. "You know, because of your disposition." I punched him in the face and heard the satisfying noise of the cartilage in his nose being radically realigned. More blood flowed out and froze the moment it hit the wing of the plane.

He took a step back from me, right to the edge of the wing as the plane started to make a slow turn onto the clear runway. I glanced for just a second at the windows; I should have shot at least one of them when I had a chance.

"I killed your bodyguards," I said, taunting him as he stood there, on the edge of the wing, watching me with those fearsome blue eyes. "Every last one of them, from Parks to Bastian."

"I know," he said, immovable, staring back at me, and I caught a flicker of something. In spite of the damage, his face wore its usual inscrutable look, but there was a hint of curl at the corner of his mouth; his version of a smile. "I am very proud of you."

"Oh, you bastard," I said and made a move for him. He dodged to his left and circled around, positioning himself between me and the fuselage of the plane. "I hope you feel the same sense of pride when I rip your soul screaming from your body."

"I would," he said quietly, "if I thought you were capable of such a thing."

"Oh, I'm capable," I said. "In case you missed it, I just coldly murdered four people that I hated way less than you, and not one of them didn't die in screaming pain."

"Indeed," he said, almost with amusement. "You have become everything I ever hoped you could be. What I made you to be—"

"YOU SON OF A BITCH!" I charged at him again and this time I connected before he could dodge. I hit him low with my shoulder into his midsection, tackling him schoolboy-style. I got astride his massive frame and scrambled up to his chest, where I proceeded to pummel his face with a punch that—no shit—caused the wing of the plane to dip. I hit him again and again and watched the cold blue eyes lose a little of their luster. "You know what you made me?" I hit him again and felt the satisfying crack of his jaw. "My mother abused and imprisoned me—Wolfe hunted and tortured me—Zack and Fries tried to seduce me for their own different reasons—and Omega and their lackeys have been dogging me every step of the way!" I hit him again. "But you— you—you ass!" I felt a hot tear run down my face as I hit him and broke his cheekbone. "You! You made me a victim." I sobbed and seethed, all in one, crying in purest fury. "For the first time ever."

I hit him again, but there was no satisfaction in it. I stopped and grew cold and looked down at his face, misshapen from what I had done to him, and I sniffed. "Now I'm gonna repay the favor."

I reached down and grabbed his face, burying my thumb in one cheek and my fingers in the other, squeezing his damaged cheekbones, feeling them crack in my grasp. I relished inflicting the pain, the righteous fury consuming me like a cold fire that would melt him to nothingness. I looked into his blue eyes, the shock of frost in there, and knew mine were colder still. "Let me show you how Zack felt," I said, pushing down on his face as though it could somehow make things work faster. You can die the way you made him die. It'll be like a little reunion. We can all be together one last time before I put an end to all of us—all of us! Once and for all."

I barely felt his hand creep up my wrist, but his grasp was far too weak to stop me. I felt the first of my power begin to work, to drain him, but he was cold to the touch in spite of the heat, a cold numbness that crept up my fingers from where they met his face. I waited, wanting it, wanting to draw him in so I could destroy us all together—all the people who had hurt me so badly, all in one convenient package, all destined for the same screaming oblivion. The top of the IDS tower seemed like a good place to do it. Or a bullet from my own gun, properly aimed.

The cold numbness in my right hand grew more fierce where I was touching him, and the haze of my power dimmed. I snapped out of the sweet haze of my power working, the drain of his soul slowing to a trickle and then stopping. I opened my eyes with a shock and realized that Winter had turned loose his power, that there was a thick layer of ice that held my hand imprisoned in his, that separated my touch from his skin, from his face. He pushed back and lifted me off him with my trapped wrist and I felt it crack where it was buried deep in the ice. He stood, forcing himself up atop his long, ungainly legs and he brought us both to standing, though he did it to me unwillingly, and the pain I felt coupled with the numb cold in my right hand was staggering enough that I couldn't ignore it.

"I see that you have forgotten," he said, as he held me at arm's length, speaking through his comically distorted and beaten face, "that you are not the only one who carries a touch that can kill." He took a deep breath of the cold air as the plane locked itself into position, ready for takeoff. "I am proud of you; you truly have become all I have wanted you to be."

"I ... will ... kill you ..." I sobbed as he bent my arm around and faced me off the back of the plane's wing.

"Perhaps," he said calmly. "But not today. Til we meet again."

Whatever defiant words I might have spat back at him were lost as he broke my right hand off as easily as snapping a piece of stemware. I heard it shatter and then I was falling, plummeting to the tarmac below as I heard the jet engines spool up and the Gulfstream rocketed down the runway. I waited, hoping he would fall from the sky before me, unable to make it back into the plane, but I saw nothing fall but the snow, now picking up, flurries coming down all around me as the plane disappeared into the clouds.

I lay in the middle of the runway, cradling the stump where my hand had been only a moment earlier, and rocked back and forth until the pain claimed me into blissful blackness, and the snow-flecked sky was replaced by the dark of unconsciousness.

Twenty-one

I was in memories and dreams again, and this time I knew it. Zack was there, striding through a hallway as fast as he could go. His pace was good, he walked quickly, and the insubstantial ghost of me was dragged along for the ride. I recognized where we were; it was Headquarters at the Directorate. Outside, the skies were dark. Ahead was a light and an office that was eminently familiar—Old Man Winter's, and the bastard himself was behind the desk, dressed exactly as he had been on the night the Directorate had been destroyed.

The night Zack had died.

Zack knocked on the doorframe; it was mere formality, but Old Man Winter looked up from what seemed to be a daze. He blinked at Zack, at the sound, then cocked his head and regarded him curiously as Zack spoke. "You called me, sir?"

Winter seemed to regain his mental footing. "Status?" he rumbled.

"Campus is clear, sir," Zack said. "Our remaining metas are clumped together in the dorm, all non-essential personnel are evacuated, and all is quiet."

Old Man Winter only gave a slight nod that he had heard or cared what Zack had said, but his expression suddenly shifted to something more curious. "You have ... become intimate with Sienna."

Zack flushed. "You've been spying on her? On us?"

"Always." Winter waited for his reaction.

"I thought you'd given that up now that she's been working for you for nearly a year," Zack said.

Old Man Winter cocked his head at an off angle. "That I keep an eye on prized assets should hardly come as a surprise to you."

Zack's face got twisted, resentful. "Like I said to you months ago; I'm not telling you anything about our relationship anymore."

"It is true," Winter acknowledged, "you have not been of much help lately in determining her state of mind. I have hoped that would change."

"Doubtful," Zack said, gritting his teeth. "If there was any way I could find to tell her what I did when she and I first got started—if I could expose you and the fact that you're still spying on her without completely burning my bridge to her in the process?" He looked away. "Be assured I'd do it." There came a change over Zack's expression. "I'm in love with her. And I won't let anything come between the two of us nor allow any harm to come to her."

Old Man Winter showed little reaction. "A bold proclamation. You are the tie that binds her to this place, to us. You've done better than I ever would have predicted; but let us admit it, she has other friends she relies on now, a burgeoning support mechanism."

"Barely, now," Zack said. "Reed and Scott gone, Kat incapacitated—I'm all she's got left."

Old Man Winter didn't flinch. "True enough." He leaned forward. "You must speak with her on a matter of critical importance."

Zack's skepticism immediately showed. "What?"

Old Man Winter's eyes flickered. "Her reluctance to kill is becoming a liability."

Zack snorted. "You talk about her in terms of assets and liabilities, like she's just some number on a balance sheet that needs to be shifted around." He glared at Winter. "If she's that easy to figure out, why not shift her into the 'kill' column yourself?" He waited for a response. "You know why you can't?"

Winter gave no hint of emotion. "She has fears—"

"It's not that," Zack said with a smug smile. "You'll never guess, probably because you were never like her." The smile faded, replaced with an almost haunted look. "It's because she's got a good heart." He smiled again, bitterly this time. "Cheesy as that sounds, everything done to her over the years just damaged the surface; it didn't kill off her ability to feel. She looks in the eyes of people and she still feels like they're people, not just items under her control. In spite of what everyone's tried to do to her, in spite of that snarky defense mechanism she fires off every few seconds that keeps almost everyone at a distance, she cares more about people than I think you ever did." Zack folded his arms. "You probably don't understand that, though."

Winter took a long breath, and when he breathed it out the air in front of him frosted. "Better than you know."

"I don't want her to be a killer," Zack said, staring him down. "I don't want her to be like you—like us, always seeing people in the way they can be moved, pushed or taken out of the way if needed. I want her to be herself. I want her to *keep* being herself— good heart and all. Killing a person coarsens you in ways she shouldn't have to experience." He glared at Winter. "I bet if you do it enough, you can just about lose your whole soul."

Whatever might have been said next was lost as a sudden flash lit the windows. The lights blinked off then on and finally went dead. There was an explosion outside and the building shook, and Zack's gun was in his hand even as Old Man Winter was on his feet. Steps were audible outside the office and Ariadne was there a moment later, along with M-Squad—all of whom must have been in her office. I looked at the faces of them—Bastian and Parks solemn, Clary a little excited, and Eve emotionless—the faces of people who were now dead, people that I'd killed.

"It's starting," Parks said, rather futilely, I thought. Another explosion followed his words, the fixtures of headquarters rattling in the shockwave. "They're here."

"We must—" Old Man Winter began to speak but stopped, his eyes frozen as he looked past the members of M-Squad who were clustered just outside his office door.

"Hello, Eric," a shadowy figure came forward out of the darkness, her greeting tempered by a heavy accent. There was a multiplicity of shadowy figures standing out in the cubicle farm that monopolized the center of the fourth floor, none of them visible in anything other than silhouette save for the one who had spoken, the one who stood in the aisle that led straight out Winter's door. She stepped forward another step, and the explosions out the windows to her left lit her face. She was barely visible, even with the fading glow of the explosion that had destroyed the science building lighting her profile.

"Bastet," Winter said, shouldering his way past Zack and M-Squad. "It has been a long time since Bubastis. I can only assume that this is not a social call."

"Hardly," she said with dull amusement, almost slinking forward, holding to the shadows. "We've come to destroy your Directorate, all the buildings, all the structures and, if you force us to, you as well."

"And what have we done that has so provoked Omega's ire, Bast?" I could have sworn I heard a little sarcasm from him.

"As if you don't know," she said, laughing. She didn't act particularly venerable, the way I would have thought an old god would; she seemed more cautious. "Stealing Andromeda and allowing her to be killed by Century?"

Winter showed a flicker of emotion. "Century? I had thought them finished long ago."

Bastet offered him a playful smile. "You are far behind, Erich. They're a threat, rising in power, growing. They have new leaders—one them I think you're very familiar with—what was his name when you ran across him in Peshtigo?"

Winter actually paled, something I wouldn't have thought

possible for the light-skinned giant. "He called himself Sovereign. A man unto himself."

"Sovereign and Century," Bastet said, smirking. "Andromeda was our hedge against them. Sienna was too, once we found out about her, but you've blocked her from us." She gave a neat shrug. "That's fine. You've annoyed and harassed us for far too long, Winter, hampering everything we do in America to try and protect our interests. Your moment to do that is done." Her face hardened. "Century has begun wiping out every single metahuman that they can get to. They mean to destroy us all, and leave only themselves behind on the earth."

"Who are they?" Zack said, and I sensed his sudden blush when the question crept out.

Bastet smiled. "They are a hundred of the world's most powerful metas, united in a common purpose." Her smirk vanished. "To be last one hundred metas on the face of the planet."

"Extinction of the species?" Parks said. "I can't believe the humans are just gonna lie down and let themselves get wiped out."

"The humans will not be wiped out," Bastet said. "They'll be slaves."

"Ridiculous," Zack said. "A hundred metas against the armies of the world? Against guns, and bombs and nuclear weapons?" He snorted. "Good luck. Your age was over about a millennium ago." He looked her up and down. "That cat ... is out of the bag."

Bastet laughed at his joke, a delicate, chiming laugh that was followed with something that almost sounded like the meow of a mountain lion. "I'm afraid that until fairly recently, you would have been right. The relentless march of technology has dissolved our advantage over the humans. That was made painfully obvious to us who believed differently by the chaos of World War One." She turned her gaze to Winter, who had said nothing. "But with the addition of ... Sovereign ... at their head ... you are now quite wrong."

"He …" Winter said, "… has never cared to involve himself in the affairs of others. He has never desired to bother with anything he did not wish to … dabble with."

Bastet's eyes flicked narrow, like a cat, watching them. "It would appear that someone has changed his mind." She waved a hand at them, Zack, Ariadne, who stood still, too stunned to speak, and M-Squad. "None of you need die right now. My orders are to destroy your facilities and warn you to remove yourselves from our affairs. Interfere with us again, it will become rather more than warning, but for now … every last one of you can walk out of here today, go on about the rest of your lives free from worry." She smiled. "Other than the worry that should creep upon you at the thought of what Century is doing in this very moment. And the fear of what we will do should you come between us and our objectives again." She looked them over with a smile. "Go on. Be about your business. Omega will take care of this problem." She let out a slow breath that sounded like she was stretching. "Just as we always have."

With that, she started to recede into the darkness. "Oh, and by the way, Erich … Sienna Nealon will be joining us."

Winter was stone, a monolith taller than any of the others in the room. "Sienna will make her own decisions."

Bastet smiled again, and I could sense the infuriating effort she put into it. "Of course. But her decision will be to come with us, eventually. And woe betide he who stands between us and our goals, you remember that, right?" She looked him over carefully. "Of course not. You always were a slow learner, Erich." She snapped her fingers. "Remind him. Roughly, if necessary." She turned and started to stride out, and the other shadows, the ones that had surrounded her, they remained, and began to move closer to the office, to M-Squad, to Zack.

I felt myself pulled out of the memory, back to a place of cold, of pain. It felt like I had fallen, and when I landed it was roughly, on the runway at the airport in Eden Prairie. I felt the searing agony of my lost hand and the cold air filled my sinuses. I remembered what had happened, where I was, and the tears streamed down my face as a presence came over me. "I'm sorry, Zack. I'm sorry I couldn't kill him for you."

It's okay. I never wanted you to. I never wanted you to be a killer. I just wanted you to be you. I love you.

"I know," I said. "I know. I'm sorry I doubted you."

You have to get up now.

There were sirens in the distance, I could hear them, wailing loud and growing closer. *You have to get up,* Zack said again. *You have to get out of here before they arrive.*

"Yes," I said, "okay." I dragged myself to my knees, spasms of pain racking me in between the occasional sob. I started toward the fence in the distance, the one I had entered the airport over, and I started running, tuning out the pain. "You're with me. You're finally with me."

Yeah. Sorry it took me so long. I was afraid. Afraid you'd find out what I did. How we started. I was afraid that you'd never forgive me.

"I forgive you," I sobbed, running through the snowy night. "I forgive you." I sniffed. "There's only one person I can't forgive, and it's not you."

I kept running until I got to the fence, and by the time I had cleared it and gotten back to my car, the wind had numbed me, numbed my pain—everything but the little bit still inside, hiding, secreted away with Zack.

Twenty-two

I made it a few miles down the road before I stopped. I pulled off Minnesota Highway 62 at the exit for Southdale Mall. I kept going down the snow-covered surface roads until I pulled into the parking lot of the mall. I figured I had gone far enough, that this was good enough for what I had in mind. *Glove box,* Zack's voice told me, and I opened it to find what I needed. I swallowed heavily; we were close to the end now. We had to be.

I stepped out into the night air and let the chill wash over me. Not much farther now. I went to the trunk, ignoring the snowflakes, and let my bare hand trail over the cold exterior of the car. It made my fingers numb, which was how I wanted them. I took a breath as I stood over the trunk, not really ready for what I was about to do. It opened and I stared down.

Ariadne lay within, bound with duct tape around her mouth, her hands and her feet. She let her eyes flick open, and when she saw me, it was a thousand megawatts of SCREW YOU evident in her eyes.

"Time to go, Ariadne," I said, and cut the tape around her hands, then her feet. The silk bathrobe that still covered her was barely adequate, but I tried to help her wrap it around herself before I pulled her out. She stared at me, huddling against the chill. I took off my coat and offered it to her as she shivered in the winter air. I saw her hesitate, and I knew she was thinking about telling me to stick it. She made the wise choice in the end, though, and put it on.

"Is she dead?" she asked me after a moment's silence.

"Yes."

"Are you happy now?" There was more than a little accusation in how she said it.

There was a pause before I answered her. "No. Happiness seems like a pretty far off dream at this point, like something I might have woken up to a long time ago. Not something that exists in my reality anymore." I shrugged, and she stood there, indifferent, shivering against the cold. "What about you? Eve clubbed you unconscious and hauled you away from the scene of the crime, but I still caught you with her. You even saved her life—for a little while, anyway." I leaned in closer and I saw her flinch. "Are you happy, Ariadne? Did being with her make you happy enough to overlook what she did?"

"I ..." Ariadne swallowed heavily, and clenched the coat tighter. Her bare feet looked cold in the snow, but I had reached the limit of what I was willing to give her. "I loved her, you know."

"I'm not surprised."

"Love tends to allow you to overlook some things, yes," Ariadne said harshly. "Foolish things, maybe. Maybe it made me stupid, to try and ignore it, to be with her in spite of it, but—"

"Oh, enough," I said. "You overlooked murder. Your pals were all killers. Cold-blooded. You overlooked the fact that they stood there, and held me down, and made me use my own body to kill Zack. Sure, you were all upset in the moment, but Eve just whistles at you and you came running back, like a loyal b—-"

"You don't know anything about me," Ariadne said, and I heard her voice crack.

"Ditto," I spat back at her. "Best of luck." I turned and started to get back in the car.

"Where does it end, Sienna?" Ariadne called out. "You killed them all, didn't you?"

"Not Winter," I said, stopping myself, the door open. "I got all of them but Winter."

"And once he's dead?" she asked. "What will you do then?"

"I don't know." I shrugged. The wind howled, pulling against the door of the car as if it were trying to rip it from the hinges. "Does it matter?"

"There's a lot going on out there," Ariadne said. "This thing, this storm that's coming … it's bigger than any of us. Bigger than you and me, you and Winter—"

"It's a little late in our relationship for you to be trying to give me career counseling," I replied. "I think we passed the cutoff for that a few dead bodies—and a hell of a lot of trust—ago." I stared at her, watched her, forlorn. "Goodbye, Ariadne. There's a cell phone in the coat pocket. You can use it to call a friend to come and get you."

There was a long, stark moment of silence. "I don't have any left," she said, and it was a bitter, frail statement of a truly lonely person.

I lowered myself into the seat and started the engine. "Join the club." I closed the door behind me and pushed the accelerator pedal, and watched as she began to disappear in the rearview mirror. I stopped after a moment, and looked instead at the imposing structure of the mall, lit up all around me.

I turned to follow the ring road around the mall parking lot, but hit the brakes when I came around a corner. Everything looked desperately familiar, and it took only a moment for me to remember why. I'd never been inside this mall, nor around it, really, and there was a reason for that. I had seen it, though, from a distance. From a news chopper's camera view of what was happening around it.

It was where Wolfe had slaughtered dozens of people while trying to get me to come out and face him.

I stared at the spot in the parking lot where I remembered watching him cut through a SWAT team like they were wet sandwich bread being shredded by a hungry bird, and I felt a pang in my guts. Wolfe stirred within me, his dark excitement obvious as he relived his kills—the smells of the event, the sights of it, the screams. I could feel Bjorn as well, less excited and more indifferent. Gavrikov watched quietly, and though they were newly with me, I could feel Eve and Bastian back there, somewhere, acclimating to their new surroundings.

"I'm never going to be able to undo all the damage that's been done on my behalf, am I?" I didn't know who would answer me, but I had hopes.

Not your fault, Zack said.

"It's like a nightmare I can't wake up from," I said, and leaned against the steering wheel. "People die for me—because of me. I finally got to the point where I was trying to make a life, and I was trying to protect ... the world, to be ... I don't know, what I thought Winter wanted me to be ... and it turns out he just wanted to make me into one of you ..." I sent the furious word accusingly into my depths, and felt it reverberate there among the ones I cast it at, "... and now I am. I'm one of you. I'm no protector. I don't help police metas. All I am is a killer."

There is no shame in killing to good cause, Bjorn said. *Only in bad cause—*

"As if you would know the difference."

There is a threat growing, Gavrikov said. *I put aside my worries for it to pursue rumors of Klementina, but it does exist. It is out there.*

"Century," I breathed, and felt every last one of them agree with me. "Sovereign."

They will destroy the world of metahumans, to the last, Bjorn said, *and then enslave humanity, with Sovereign at their head.* I could feel his fear, tingling inside me, so powerful it almost made me quiver. *He is the most powerful meta on the planet.*

"Why do you need me?" I felt the faux leather of the steering wheel against my forehead. "Why me? Why did all this have to happen ... for me?"

There was a moment's quiet. *I do not know,* Bjorn said. *But I know someone who does. And so do you.*

I felt a steely calm settle over me, and I sat back up, lifting my head off the wheel. I looked at that empty space in the parking lot in front of me, one more time. It was covered over completely with snow now, streaming heavily from overhead. I wondered if there was a stain underneath, something, anything to show what had happened there. It felt like there should be a reminder, so that others could mark the passage of my failures. The snow kept on, though, covering the place where more people had died for me while I failed to act, kept going and going, burying it like my sins, until I finally put the car back into gear and started driving—as if I could leave all those sins behind me.

Twenty-three

It was dark, and there was an aura of cologne in the room. It didn't quite gag me, but it was close, and I tried to decide whether it was because I hated cologne in general or this cologne in particular. I leaned toward the latter but didn't much care either way. My fingers ran across the smooth leather arms of the chair I sat in, waiting. I wasn't in much danger of falling asleep, but by the same token I wasn't exactly well-rested, especially lately. The dark living room sprawled out in front of me, and I had a clear line of sight to the front door.

I heard the key hit the lock and turn it, along with muffled talking, soft murmuring through the wood. When it opened, the front porch light cast a thin shaft of illumination into the room, almost to the foot of my chair. There was the silhouette of a man and a woman, entwined, his lips on hers. She broke away for a moment, and started to say something, but he went back in for another kiss and she acquiesced, staying locked with him like that for a few seconds until I saw her go limp in his arms. He let her hang like that while he shut the door. "Thank God," I heard him mutter to her, "I thought you'd never shut up."

"You are such a charmer, James," I said, and I saw him freeze in the entry. He flipped the light and I stared at him, gun in hand. "It amazes me that women continue to fall for your palaver."

James Fries stood there, his best attempt at a brave, almost cocky smile on his face. "You did, once upon a time, as I recall."

"I was young and stupid," I said.

"It was like three months ago."

"Very good," I said sarcastically, "keep insulting the woman who has a gun pointed at you and hasn't hesitated to shoot you in the past. The sad thing is," I said with a nasty smile, "you won't even be the first person I've killed this week. And believe it or not, I liked all the others more than I like you. By a lot."

There was a pause as he seemed to take stock of the situation, surveying his surroundings as if it were the first time he had seen his own home. "What do you want?" I saw his Adam's apple bulge as he swallowed. I could almost hear the comical GULP as he did it.

The woman at his feet stirred, her eyes blinking. She had dark hair and bright eyes, ones that were barely visible as she slit them shut. "What … happened?"

"You slipped," I said, "and went home with a real dickhead." I lowered the gun to the side of the chair, where she couldn't see it.

She blinked at me, then frowned. "Who are you?" She looked up at Fries, then back at me. "Wait … are you married?"

I felt the burst of revulsion but ignored it. "Get out of here," I told her coldly.

She dragged herself upright, swaying as she did so. She gave Fries a scornful, pissed off look. "Asshole," she pronounced. She turned to me. "I'm sorry. He didn't tell me he was married."

I let my teeth grind together as she closed the door behind her, and then pulled the gun back into view.

"You don't need that, you know," Fries said and tried a broad grin.

I let out a noise that I could only describe as loathing giving auditory form. "I hate you. I hate you so much, that I am indeed going to start filling you with bullets the next time you speak and say something I don't want you to say." I pulled back the hammer and his eyes got wide. "I'm aiming for your groin first, then your kneecaps, and then, eventually, when I'm bored, I'll try locating that minuscule pea you use to think." I pretended to give it a moment's thought. "Wait, no, I said I was going to shoot you in the groin first, didn't I?"

I could see the strain in his face; he didn't doubt me. "What do you want?" His whole body was taut, his shoulders stiff under his snow-specked winter coat.

I took a breath and listened for the voices within. They were quiet, in agreement for once, total harmony, and I didn't know whether to be greatly comforted or greatly disturbed by that. I let out a long, slow exhale. "I want you to call Janus," I said, letting my finger play with the idea of just pulling the trigger and being done with it. I held back, letting whatever angels were left in my nature take the helm. I doubted there were many at this point. "I want you to call him and tell him to get his ass over here, right now.

"I'm ready to talk."

Epilogue

The office was wood-paneled, extravagant, something out of a bygone era, but the man who now inhabited it was, by his own reckoning, something very different. He took a deep breath of the air and smelled the remains of a thousand cigars that had been smoked within its walls. The old, leather-bound tomes one might expect in such an august setting lined bookshelves from one end of the office to the other and had undoutedly absorbed the smoky smell, taking it into the very fibers of their pages. The young man who sat in the high-backed leather chair behind the old wooden desk at the center of that office hadn't read a single one of those books, but he knew they were old; some of them were first editions of great works of literature and historical pieces in their own right. A collector's dream. He took another breath of the air—it just smelled old to him—and drummed his fingers idly on the desk.

The tall, dark-skinned woman who sat opposite him wore a faint smile. He didn't know if it was genuine, but he assumed it was. Who wouldn't be pleased at a moment like this, after all? It was a time of change, time for something new. And for an organization as old as Omega, that took some doing.

Street lamps shone in behind him, the dark of night broken by the quiet glow from outside. He knew the sun would be coming up soon. It was an adjustment for him, still living on Pacific Time and moving to Greenwich Mean Time, but he'd cope. It'd be worth it, after all.

"Bastet," he said. The woman across from him looked up at him with her dark eyes, and he caught a glimmer of a chastened cat as he looked at her. "It's gonna be a great day, you know."

Her reserve kept her from being as excited as he was. That was forgivable. "It certainly has the potential to be, Primus."

There was a quiet ring of the phone on his desk, and he snatched it up, only fumbling it a little as Bastet watched him. "Yo," he said into the receiver; it was an old thing, not modern at all, but at least it had a speakerphone. "Okay. Put him on." He looked across the desk at Bastet. "Janus is calling. Won't he be surprised?"

He punched the button for the speaker and waited, a subtle hiss filling the air. After a moment there was a crackle, and then a tired voice at the other end of the line. "Hello?" it said, thickly accented.

"J," he called toward the phone as he set the receiver down, "it's Rick."

There was a moment's pause on the other end of the phone, and Rick caught Bastet's eye—they both knew Janus was trying to reconcile what he'd just heard. "I need to speak with your father," Janus said, his voice strained.

"Got a bad news/good news situation for you there, J. Dad's dead." Rick kept his eyes on Bast, though he didn't know what for. Janus and his father were oldest friends; it wasn't like he'd be happy to hear that Rick was sitting in the big chair now, after all.

"Dead?" Janus's warm tones were knit with reaction, but it was subtle.

"Yeah, he kicked off a couple days ago," Rick said with calm assurance. "No one really saw it coming, but I jumped a jet from L.A. the moment I heard and came back. The ministers confirmed me as Primus this evening." He let a little smile peek through; was it wrong to be a little excited? He'd been waiting to inherit this post all his life. It was all he'd ever wanted. The pause on the other end of the phone was annoying, though. "J? You still there?"

"Yes," Janus's smooth cadences came through the crackling

of the receiver. The old phone would have to go. So would all the old stuff—the books, the paintings of ships and old gods, the sculptures of things from the old world. Maybe even the behemoth of a desk that looked painfully large, as if a ship had sailed into the middle of the office and dumped it off. "I am still here, merely trying to … come to terms with the painful news you have just broken."

"He was old, J," Rick said. "He'd lived thousands of years. This isn't exactly a surprise."

"I spoke with him not two weeks ago," Janus said. "He seemed to be in fine health at the time."

"Things change fast," Rick said with a shrug at Bast. What was the point of dwelling on what was done? "Keep up, okay? Now, we need to talk. I know Dad had you working on this Sienna Nealon thing. This slow and steady crap plainly ain't working. We need to get results now—"

"About that," Janus interrupted, and Rick felt his face go slack. Best not to show the hired help his irritation. He was a leader now, in charge. There'd be time to correct bad behaviors later. "I have received a call from our agent in Minneapolis. Ms. Nealon has requested a meeting."

Rick laid his head back against the stuffed, padded chair. It was damned comfortable. Maybe the only thing from the old office he would keep. He let his eyes flit around, briefly. If the aesthetics allowed for it. If they didn't, it'd be in the dump with all the rest of the stuff that didn't belong anymore. "Really? Dad told me about your plans. I thought he was crazy to back that play."

There was a hiss of static from the phone and a long hesitation before a reply came. "Apparently not," Janus's voice came through at last. "Though this did happen faster than I had anticipated."

"Well, how about that?" Rick said with quiet amusement. "All right, good on you. Never let it be said I won't own up to it when I'm wrong; that's not the kind of leader I am. So you've got a meeting with her. Good. Now get her back here."

There was almost no pause this time. "I will do what I can, but we have to keep in mind that Ms. Nealon is particularly headstrong, and to rush ourselves in this moment would be foolhardy given how much effort we have spent cultivating our opportunities to lead to this. To have played so subtly up to now, trying to build trust and win her confidence so that she will listen and come to embrace our plans—I don't wish to throw it away by becoming impatient."

"Yeah, yeah," Rick waved his hand dismissively at the phone. If Janus had been here, dismissing him was exactly what he would have done. Did the man not understand the importance of results in this situation? "We need her now. We need to move up the timetable. I just got briefed by our intel guys, and they say that Century has got units in Europe, the Middle East and Africa right now. You know what that means, right?"

"They have begun to spread to the rest of the world." Janus got it. That was good. It was easier to be a leader when you weren't surrounded by total idiots.

"Right you are," Rick said with a tight smile. "They've been working Russia and the Far East for a while now, but they're crossing borders and moving faster. They're widening the net, they're expanding, and the body count is soaring. They've got hunters in the field, J. Humans and metas, and they're sweeping it clean. We need Nealon. We've got a playbook with a few things that might work, but you know we need her to run the best damned play." Rick didn't want to hear hesitation in the response, but it was there. "J ... you're not having ... doubts ... are you?" The word doubts came close to being breathed like a curse. Rick wasn't the kind of leader that liked second thoughts.

"Your father and I had many discussions about how best to proceed when he brought me back to advise him," Janus said. "I will tell you the same thing that I told him—that what we are trying to do now is dangerous. That I acknowledge because of circumstances beyond our control that changes have to be made in to our ways, things codified into unspoken law for us for millennia. That I believe we are in very real danger of creating bigger problems if we were to—"

"J, I think you're misunderstanding me," Rick said with a smile and a shake of his head. Sure, Janus couldn't see his expression, but he could hear it, right? Maybe even feel it, given his power? Rick frowned. The idea of Janus being able to use that power was concerning. But it only worked on the weak willed, wasn't that what his father had told him? Rick felt himself relax. Weak will wasn't a problem for him. "I'm not intending to do anything to disrupt the way we've handled these things for thousands of years. What I'm planning to do is what my father called Plan B." There was a quiet on the other end of the phone. "J? Are you being coy with me?"

"No," Janus said. "So you mean to remove Sovereign from the equation?"

"Without Sovereign," Rick said with dry satisfaction, "Century is nothing."

"I disagree," Janus said, "I think they will be much reduced in their effectiveness, however, without him."

"Potato, potah-toe," Rick said. "Either way, we need to take Sovereign off the board. Sienna Nealon's our path to that. Get her over here."

"I will," Janus said stiffly. "I may need some time, though—"

"Time's not a luxury we're afforded right now," Rick said, and his eyes fixed on Bastet. She was thousands of years old, had been more powerful than most men he'd met in Omega. She was still a good -looking woman, though, worthy of the statues that had once been made for her. He knew he could have her, really, in his guts. That was power. Real power. "Get her to London.

However you have to. If she won't come willingly, I will send overwhelming force against her, and we will beat her down and drag her here."

"I would caution you against that," Janus said. "She does not respond well to pressure."

"To hell with how she responds," Rick said. He cast one last look around the office before turning his attention back to this conversation. He felt a swell of weariness. Must be bedtime in L.A. "Get her over here, or I will. And either way, however it happens, once Sienna Nealon comes to London—to Omega—she will never be allowed to leave again."

Author's Note

Let me start off by saying that I know that was short. Sorry for that, and I can promise that I'll make it up to you with book 7, which is not even halfway written and already as long as this volume. It should end up being the biggest Girl in the Box book yet, if that's any consolation. This was a necessarily quick and brutal part of Sienna's story, but now that that is over with, it's time for her to start moving on as we gear up for the last four books. That's right, only four more to the end of the series (I added the titles to the list of my books a couple of pages from now, after the preview for book seven. If you want to know as soon as the next volumes are released, to sign up for my mailing list. I promise I won't spam you (I only send an email when I have a new book released) and I'll never sell your info. You can also unsubscribe at any time.

Thanks for going on the journey with me thus far. I know, you're here for Sienna, not me, but still, thank you. I'm going to do everything I can to make her conclusion worthy of the story thus far. If you've enjoyed the books, I'd appreciate it if you'd take the time to write a short review wherever you purchased this book. Thanks for reading, and I hope to see you again next time.

Robert J. Crane

About the Author

Robert J. Crane was born and raised on Florida's Space Coast before moving to the upper midwest in search of cooler climates and more palatable beer. He graduated from the University of Central Florida with a degree in English Creative Writing. He worked for a year as a substitute teacher and worked in the financial services field for seven years while writing in his spare time. He makes his home in the Twin Cities area of Minnesota.

He can be contacted in several ways:
Via **email** at cyrusdavidon@gmail.com
Follow him on **Twitter** – @robertJcrane
Connect on **Facebook** – robertJcrane (Author)
Website – http://www.robertJcrane.com
Blog – http://robertJcrane.blogspot.com
Become a fan on **Goodreads** –
http://www.goodreads.com/RobertJCrane

Sienna Nealon will return in

ENEMIES
THE GIRL IN THE BOX, BOOK SEVEN

Far from home, having failed in her quest to kill Old Man Winter, Sienna Nealon finds herself in the city of London, working with Omega, her oldest enemies. Surrounded by people she doesn't trust, thrust into events that could mean the extinction of the metahuman race, Sienna will discover that the line between friend and foe is thinner than she ever could have believed - and that her greatest enemies may lie within.

Coming Autumn 2013

The Sanctuary Series
Epic Fantasy by Robert J. Crane

Defender: The Sanctuary Series, Volume One
Avenger: The Sanctuary Series, Volume Two
Champion: The Sanctuary Series, Volume Three
Crusader: The Sanctuary Series, Volume Four*
Thy Father's Shadow: A Sanctuary Novel*
Savages: A Sanctuary Short Story
A Familiar Face: A Sanctuary Short Story

The Girl in the Box
Contemporary Urban Fantasy by Robert J. Crane

Alone: The Girl in the Box, Book 1
Untouched: The Girl in the Box, Book 2
Soulless: The Girl in the Box, Book 3
Family: The Girl in the Box, Book 4
Omega: The Girl in the Box, Book 5
Broken: The Girl in the Box, Book 6
Enemies: The Girl in the Box, Book 7*
Legacy: The Girl in the Box, Book 8*
Revelations: The Girl in the Box, Book 9*
Power: The Girl in the Box, Book 10*

Forthcoming